Underneath the Moon

4

DAN HOLT
and
MAX HOLT

Published by:

MaxHoltMedia

DAN HOLT & MAX HOLT

OTHER SCI-FI BOOKS BY DAN HOLT
Underneath the Moon
Underneath the Moon 2
Underneath the Moon 3
Keepsake
Sleep Mode
(The above releases are also on Kindle
    and Audio, via Audible)
Coming soon...**UTM4,** the **Audio Edition**

Intended future releases –
        Underneath The Moon 5 & 6

OTHER SCI-FI BOOKS BY MAX HOLT
Alien Planet
Series Under development:
            AI Rising

Cover design by Max Holt Media, with Eddie Holt

ISBN: 13: 978-1-944537-27-2

Published by: Max Holt Media
303 Cascabel Place,
Mount Juliet, TN 37122
www.maxholtmedia.com
On facebook at www.facebook.com/maxholtmedia
      Email – max@maxholtmedia.com
      Twitter - @maxholtmedia

A NOTE FROM THE AUTHOR

I had planned for the story, Underneath the Moon, to stand as a trilogy. However, I received a comment from a reader, for which I am grateful, suggesting that this story, as told in the three volumes, be a world-building saga that will encompass many volumes.

In thinking that through, much untold intrigue and adventure comes to mind; an opportunity to speculate on a possible future.

What is *really out there*?

So, in this volume and those to follow, come journey with the giants and the *little ones* to the stars; deeper into the cosmos, to the many mysteries yet to unfold.

I am glad to have my brother *and my publisher*, Max Holt, join me to co-author the continuing **Underneath the Moon** saga. As a retired military officer, he will bring a unique perspective as the *little ones* head toward the stars.

Dan Holt

CONTENTS

DAN HOLT & MAX HOLT

PROLOGUE

June 2, 2036 - Easter Island
4000 feet under the sea

The Leviathan, a science vessel, the latest and most powerful research tool for undersea exploration, was commissioned by the U.S. Navy to explore the waters around Easter Island. The deployment was driven by an unusual event.

Earlier, a Navy Survey aircraft had been sonar-mapping the ocean floor when it picked up low-level signals emanating from under the sea floor, a sea floor under 4000 feet of water. The airborne craft was unable to pinpoint the signal's location. The signal ceased and it was logged as an **Unknown Anomaly**.

Then, six months later, purely by happenstance, a U.S. Navy submarine, sailing the waters near Easter Island, picked up a duplicate signal with identical content and duration, but with much greater strength. A full investigation was ordered and the Leviathan entered the picture.

The research vessel's powerful equipment was able to record what its Skipper deemed *impossible.* The researchers forwarded their findings to the office of Admiral Irwin Waddell, head of the US Navy's Cyber-War Research Center, and then waited for instructions.

After reading the Leviathan's report, Admiral Waddell's mind went back to an event he had studied as a Plebe in the Naval Academy. He turned to his computer and searched the Cloud for, *Professor Charles Liggins*. After a moment, the summary of a report written by the late Professor twenty-six years earlier, appeared. The report had been written shortly after the giants, who had been discovered on the moon in the late twentieth century, had left for Alpha Centauri and their original home; the planet, Zannia. The Admiral focused on the screen as he read:

*"In the year 1998, a lone six-passenger research vessel, **Research One**, powered by a new breakthrough in propulsion, journeyed to the moon to research suspected ruins on its surface. It was discovered that those ruins, made of solid glass, were remnants of a retirement community of an ancient culture. NASA, obviously for political reasons, did not report the find. The ruins had been undetectable from Earth, using standard telescope technology.*

Also, in their search, they discovered an underground tunnel and lab from that civilization, and quite unexpectedly, 1600 giant humanoids that had been put in suspended animation. The most astounding 'find' was a NASA Apollo astronaut, in one of the giant's suspended animation units. He had been marooned, purposely left behind, by his fellow astronaut, in an attempt to keep the moon's secret from the people of Earth. The mission brought him home to be reunited with his family, causing the government to face scrutiny from an angry public and Congress.

Following those awkward revelations and adjustments, planet Earth went into action and managed to revive 1216 of the beings and bring them to Earth. It was eventually discovered that they were students of that culture and had been working on the moon in a Retirement Facility, caring for their elderly, as part of their academic training. They were being monitored by four adult Counselors who were also in the group of survivors.

Research revealed that an ancient disaster, some 50,000 years earlier, had destroyed their civilization. As an original body in our solar system, their home planet, Solaris 4, now known as the Asteroid Belt, had exploded. They and the youths were hurriedly hidden underground and put to sleep to save some of the members of their civilization. It was believed at that time that all other members of their civilization had perished.

NASA, working with the giants, tediously sifting through their scattered and fragmented records and possessions, discovered that their 'true home' was in the Alpha Centauri Star System, on a planet they called Zannia. Those records also revealed that, due to an impending environmental disaster on Zannia, the giants had come to our Solar System eons ago, in an enormous starship that they had christened Zannia 2. It had experienced a failure of its propulsion system and was steered into orbit around Saturn before being abandoned.

Earth, in a very unusual and timely effort, banded together, constructed a starship employing the new breakthrough in propulsion, and enabled the giants to journey back to their home planet. In exchange, Earth was given salvage rights to the Zannia 2, which contained a huge treasure of precious metals.

Before the disaster, the giants had occupied Solaris 4, Venus, Mars, and Earth's moon. Only the inhabitants of Earth, though Earth was severely damaged, survived the bombardment from the ancient explosion. It is assumed that the scientists of that culture and the government, had boarded their fleet of ships, estimated at about fifty, and fled into the cosmos, never to be heard from again."

DAN HOLT & MAX HOLT

Chapter 1

S. O. S

Aboard the Leviathan
Anchored in Hangaroa Port - Easter Island

Alan Newman, an early riser at sixty-six years old, finished dressing and headed for the galley, and coffee. He was a crew member of the Leviathan, the latest in undersea mapping and ocean floor penetrating technology. His task would start in a couple of hours. They had finished mapping the assigned area and were ready to assemble the digital files and report the results.

Alan took the long way to breakfast, out along the deck, to get some fresh morning air. He stopped mid-ship with his hand on the rail, looking at several giant Moai in the distance. *"They know something,"* he thought.

His gaze went from the statues down to the calm waters, supporting the ship. He had a gut feeling about this assignment to investigate the depths of the ocean floor around the island. He hadn't mentioned it to any of his colleagues because of what it might stir up. He could be wrong and that would not be good. But, somehow, like the Moai, *he knew.*

Many times, he had looked toward the heavens while considering the national consensus that some of the giants, who had been on Mars and the Moon, had fled into the cosmos to avoid the *disaster* eons ago.

Maybe they did. But, Alan just couldn't wrap his mind around it.

He was a young man, not long out of college, when the news of the discovery on the moon broke, and he had followed the saga of the giants closely. He knew they had to be smarter than to just fly off, helter-skelter, into an unforgiving cosmos. They had to be here; somewhere. But, where would you look? It's a big planet. But now, strange signals were detected from under the coral; beneath the Moai. Finally, knowing where to look; this had to be the ballgame. After another glance at the volcanic giants, he continued to the galley.

The Leviathan had digitally investigated the entire area around Easter Island. They had covered the ocean floor, from its undersea surface to a thousand feet down and from the base of the island to a mile out to sea. The files were now in the computer. Today was assembly and processing day. He was glad the Skipper had pulled into harbor, out of the rough seas that plagued every ship, attempting operations around the *Statue Island*. Even some hardened sailors were known to experience sea-sickness in those waters.

Alan looked forward to getting the report done so he and others on the crew could make the three-mile round-trip to Hanga Roa, the capital city. The Te Moana had the best baked fish on the island. The restaurant also sported two statues at its entrance, to greet its limited number of guests. One statue was of the Moai, that dotted the circumference of the island. The other was of the Moon People; the giants discovered on the moon. The similarities between the two were…*interesting*. He had been to Ahu Tongariki twice to get a close look at the 15 Moai, standing at attention there. Usually, such a sight always turned his eyes toward the sky. But now, he felt sure it was time to look in a different direction.

Atlantic Ocean – Off the Coast of Argentina

Admiral Kartolov, sipping his morning tea from the perch of his Fleet Commander's chair on the bridge of the newest Russian aircraft carrier, was proud to command the **Vladimir Putin.** It was the pride of the fleet. This, being its first mission since sea trials, was sure to make the Russian people proud. The Americans had been filled with what he deemed to be *false pride*, since their *discovery* and then their refusal to share the bounty the moon-giants had afforded decades ago. As a young Naval Officer, he remembered how Russia had to settle for a few trinkets and a token of crew-member positions onboard the *mostly* American-staffed vessels transiting to Mars and Saturn, recovering the Zannia 2 bounty. However, the Russians had just as much of a head for business as the Americans. Nothing personal, then. Russia had purchased several tons of the precious metals, at a stately discount.

But now, the rumbling massive hunk of steel beneath him brought a sense of equality; even superiority. From the air, the **Putin** looked like a perfect metal circle, floating in the ocean, the rotor pods making an elongated flight deck no longer a necessity. The semicircular side-deck panels had been raised to show the Argentines how impressive Russia's newest carrier was. The fleet had gotten underway so quickly that the panels had not yet been lowered to their stowed position alongside the ship, which would allow an increase to maximum speed.

The Russian looked out at the flight deck, littered with the latest and finest in fighter aircraft...all rotor pod equipped. His higher command still had some resentment toward the Americans but the Admiral was no fool; the rest of the world's militaries had already gone with the pods. It quickly became evident that the machines, so equipped, were clearly superior.

Now, with pod-equipped aircraft, the ship could be smaller overall, making it less of a target. Most impressive was the curved steel panels that could be extended upward from the outer edge of the circular deck, creating a partial dome over the ship to protect from attack. Copying the Americans' technology, observation drones could be launched from small bays along the circumference of the dome, capable of tracking and reporting on enemy aircraft and ships, two hundred miles out. The fighter aircraft could launch through bay doors on the dome or straight up, out through the top.

A sounding chime drew his attention back inside the Bridge. The aging commander checked his watch as his aide poured him another tea. He knew well why the Americans had dispatched the Leviathan so quickly; the Russian sensors had just picked up the same strange readings. *"We won't be left behind this time!"* He assured himself.

"Grosky?" The Admiral said into the intercom.

"Aye, aye, Comrade Admiral, I just finished the computations."

"How many days?!"

"Sir, I estimate you'll see your first Moai in 5.3 days."

The Leviathan Galley

Alan Newman didn't dwell too long on the Moai and what might be in the waters below the ship. He had a job to do, so he drew his mind back to the task at hand. Pouring himself a second cup of coffee, he looked up when the other five imaging specialists came filing into the galley. The smell of breakfast filled the ship.

"Chief," Alan said, "why don't we start the upload process? The computers can work on it while we are having breakfast. The complete upload will take about two hours."

"Go ahead," the chief said. "Don't instruct the *contrasting* until we have the complete image on the touch-table. I'll be having a late breakfast. The Captain just called for a Team Chief meeting on the bridge; something from HQ."

"Yes, sir."

Alan drained his cup and then headed out the door, down the corridor, and into the imaging lab. He made his way around the eight-foot-square horizontal imaging table, sat down at the computer terminal, turned on the monitor, and typed in a code. The code would instruct the computer to upload all digital files, gathered in the last five weeks, into the imaging table. He returned to the galley to have breakfast with the rest of the Imaging Team.

When the team entered the lab, the Chief was already there, waiting for the computers to finish their work. The soundings that had lasted for five weeks were being assembled to render a coherent picture of the sea floor and what it contained, from the surface to a thousand feet down. So far, this assignment had been simply giving the correct instructions to the equipment that could *see* into the ocean floor and reveal its secrets. The actual visual would be appearing on an eight-foot horizontal viewing table shortly. Then the real... *seeing*.

The Chief looked at Alan. "When will the processing be complete?"

He checked the ship's chronometer. "Any minute now."

The Chief looked around the table at his assembled team. "Well, it seems that we're not the only ones waiting on this report. This is classified; stays in this room, for now. The Skipper got a Top-Secret message from the White House. A Russian fleet may be headed our way. They were on a visit to Argentina, to coordinate use of their deep-water port, and then they suddenly got underway, two days early.

If their fleet was headed home, they would sail north. But, they are headed south. The CIA thinks they picked up some of these signals and are headed here to try to claim some sort of international right to explore the coral for whatever they think we may have found. They've always felt *slighted* because we got all of the glory for finding the giants."

The Team Supply Specialist said, "I wondered why that Russian fishing trawler was anchored off the east coast. On our break, when we hit port, the native guy I get our supplies from took me on a tour of the Moai on the east side. Driving along the coast I saw the ship, anchored about a quarter-mile out. The guy said they couldn't be fishing because these waters have been fished-out. Have yawl noticed that there is no significant fishing fleet around here? Anyway, he said the natives all know a Russian spy ship when they see one."

The Chief continued, "It's all starting to tie together. Yesterday, one of our spy ships broke a coded message from a Russian submarine that passed through this area a couple of weeks ago. They picked up some of the same signals we've been recording. Now, the Russian Navy is steaming full-speed south, headed around the horn. They could be here in five days. When this report is finished, the President wants it sent immediately on our TS Link."

No one spoke as the team stared at the Chief.

Momentarily, the silence was broken as the sixty-four square feet of viewing space flashed brightly, went dark, came back on at normal lighting, and then scrolled several Guru-determined lines of identification. Seconds later, it was filled with images from 600 feet under the coral surrounding Easter Island. The team stared at the screen as the images registered. Alan was the first to speak.

"Oh, my God! They are still here!"

The White House

"I knew it! I had a gut feeling!" The President was reading the Top-Secret message from the Leviathan. He had been up since midnight, his sleep interrupted by the CIA Director with the news of the Russian Fleet headed toward Easter Island.

"I was just out of college, a young guy running for the Senate, the first time I met Mentar. I got elected in time to vote for the funds to build their star ship. Seeing his demeanor and his logical approach to everything, I knew the missing giants would have been like him. I always doubted that they would launch out into the *infinite* like most others thought. I just didn't know where they could be."

He paused and looked at the framed photo on the Oval Office wall. The President, fourth POTUS back, stood with the giants at the ribbon-cutting ceremony for Giant City, now being called Mentar City. The world had made quantum leaps in knowledge and technology since some young self-made magnet scientist had revolutionized travel, at every level. After the discoveries on the moon, on Mars and in Saturn orbit 40 years ago, no one could have imagined what was possible today.

CIA Director, Dana Lea, always courteous to a fault, became uncomfortable with the President's pause. She cleared her throat.

"Ah, sir... Mr. President?"

"Oh, sorry, Dana. I got caught up in the moment." He held up the message. "*This,* changes everything... *if* they are alive." He glanced back at the photo. "I won't get the camera and ceremonial scissors out just yet, but I'm betting this bunch survived, just like Mentar and his students. We had better start preparing their city, just in case."

Dana couldn't tell if *re-election thoughts* were in the back of the President's mind. The President paused long enough to sign and attach a Presidential Routing Order to the message.

"Here, get this to NASA right away."

"Yes, sir. But, what about the classification? In all my history studies about the giants, I don't remember them being given any decoding equipment for the giants' starship; Little One. NASA will have to transmit it unclassified, in the open. Within minutes the whole planet will know what we know. Of course; the Russians..."

"Ah... I get your point. Okay, have NASA delay one day. That will give me time to contact the Premier and inform him of our find. I'll tell him this is a *good will gesture*, since we are all friends of the giants. It's time they came into the fold. The world is getting smaller.

I'll offer him a token of cooperation…allow a Russian dredging company to help us with the digging."

"Yes sir, I agree. I already have a couple of agents on the island. They will keep an eye on our Eastern friends, to make sure they don't overstep their bounds."

"Good."

NASA - Houston

A message was written, describing the discovery at Easter Island. It was transmitted through a giant radio dish focused on Alpha Centauri. A follow-up commentary would be maintained on survivors, if any, when the discovery was processed, keeping Mentar and the giant civilization on Zannia informed. Mentar's disposition was generally known among the *little ones*, the humans of Earth. He would surely launch a mission to come and get the Elders who survived. He was known as a leader that did not leave loose ends. It was NASA's opinion that, after the 4.2-year delay to receive the signal and just as soon thereafter that preparations could be made, Mentar and crew would be on their way. The transit time, Zannia to Earth would go much better this time.

Over the years, Earth had received messages that Zannia's scientists, working with the ship acquired from planet Earth, had been able to greatly improve the sensor system. They multiplied its sensing range tenfold. Also, they created the Magnetic Flux Generator, a system to project a magnetic field, similar to a *force field*, around the ship that would deflect microscopic particles in the ship's flight path, thereby allowing much greater speeds through the void of space. Transit time to Earth now would be reduced from twenty-two to eight years. Mentar had previously transmitted the specs for the alterations to NASA, for implementation on Earth's fleet.

Suburban Chicago

Robert W. Sheridan sat in his home office, at his horseshoe-shaped desk, reading the note one more time. Maybe there was one more book to write. The note, emailed to him by a contact and friend at Naval Research, was about an unusual discovery at the remote Easter Island. Something was deep under the ocean, periodically sending out signals in thirty second bursts. He knew it wouldn't be long before the news hit the world-wide media stream.

Robert had served on Discovery as Chief Communications and Records Officer, up until his retirement. Then, he had become a very active writer, recording everything from during his career. He laid his hand on the books that stood as sentinels, between two bookends, on his desk and read the titles:

The Decade of the Giants: by Robert W. Sheridan

Mentar: by Robert W. Sheridan and Marvin Dean Andrews

Research One: by Robert W. Sheridan and Frank Eugene Gordon

Genius at Work: The life and times of Frank Eugene Gordon, by Robert W. Sheridan

Discovery: by Robert W. Sheridan

Little One: by Robert W. Sheridan

He had written a short story soon after the giants had left for Alpha Centauri and their home planet. In it, he had speculated about what may have happened to the missing giants' ships. Were they still here, somewhere? Only one small two-person craft had been found abandoned in the Asteroid Belt. Its hull had been breached and there were no remains on board. In view of that, it was speculated, and accepted generally, that the giants, who were elder scientists from Mars and the Moon, had boarded their fleet of ships and fled into the cosmos.

Technicians, going over the exterior of the Zannia 2, the giants' ancient ship in orbit around Saturn, discovered hangar bays located in the twenty-mile-thick protective outer hull of the mother ship. Boolean Logic determined that the hangar bays would accommodate some forty ships, each 160 feet or so in diameter, and ten cargo-type ships, 360 feet in diameter. Both hangar bays had been empty.

Robert had been to Mars, twice; to Saturn space, and to the Moon. He could smell a story, a book, and there was one here in these signals coming from underneath the earth. He picked up his phone and dialed Doug and Karen Hastings' number. Doug and Dave Henson had joined forces and were at the U S Navy's Coding Lab, studying the thirty-second transmissions received from the ocean depths at Easter Island. Obviously, they had been informed.

When he finished the call, he immediately dialed Marvin and Renee Andrews' home. Marvin answered.

"Marvin," Robert began, "have you heard about the discovery at Easter Island?"

"Yes. Chester Goldwin, the NASA Administrator called me. I thought, at the time, that those giant guys were too smart to blindly fly into space with ships not capable of making an interstellar journey."

"Well, looks like they found a sheltered place. Are you and Renee going to get active again?"

"No. We have been all over the Solar System in past years. We decided when we passed 80 to settle down to some home life and watch the show on TV and the Internet. The Cloud now has everything catalogued, so we can access it from anywhere."

Robert paused a moment. "Mentar will be here in a little over twelve years."

"Yeah, you can count on it," Marvin said. "Hopefully we will get to see him one more time. You know, all the original crew of Research One are still with us, except Isaac, Dave's dad. As far as I know, they are all doing okay, so we are probably looking at a reunion with the big guy."

"I sure hope so."

Chapter 2

The Diggers

The White House

Admiral Irwin Waddell indicated the monitor in the conference room and then began: "Mr. President, this image," he said, pointing to the screen, "is the one that was captured, processed, and transmitted to us last week by the Leviathan science vessel."

"And those circles are their ships?" President David Mitchell said. "There's a uniform pattern."

"Yes, sir; we have definitely found the giants' ships. As you know, it was assumed back then that some of the giants had fled into the cosmos when Solaris 4 exploded." Admiral Waddell gestured toward the screen. "We don't know if they are alive or dead. But, it's definitely the giants that were part of the saga that happened over thirty years ago. These ships were parked here 50,000 years ago to survive the maelstrom and as the eons passed the coral covered them and eventually buried them 600 feet deep in the ocean floor.

"We believe that they are now in suspended animation, because the ships are parked here in an organized pattern. There are ten larger ships evenly spaced around Easter Island. Then the other forty smaller ships are grouped around them. Note the lines connecting the small ships to the larger ones. It's as if

25

they parked the armada and went into suspended animation. Our people speculated that the giants used laser equipment to carve out the giant statues, the Moai, and erect them on the island as a sentinel: saying, '*here we are.*' They then put themselves to sleep, not knowing how long it would take to be rescued.

"That line of thinking is supported by the account from the lunar discovery, that the giants resemble the Moai. There's evidence that the ancestors of the indigenous peoples that occupy the Island even now, copied and erected additional Moai for some time, long ago, then finally gave it up.

"Mr. President, this will be the most challenging task we have ever undertaken. We will need a hundred million dollars to dig up the ships and whoever is inside them."

"Well," President Mitchell said, "It looks like we are going to get in on the giant thing that gripped the world three decades ago."

"Perhaps, sir. It depends on whether their suspended animation systems lasted long enough. We had no idea that they were there all these years."

"Well, Gentlemen, we have no choice. Let's dig them up. How long will it take?"

"Nine dredging operations, simultaneously; between two and three years. Once we are set up, we can have one of the ships out in about three months."

"OK, but make sure one of the dredging operations is subcontracted to the Russians…add one if you have to. I made a promise to Moscow, to smooth some feathers…keep the international peace.

"You know that a Russian fleet, under the command of Admiral Kartolov, is arriving there today. The Russians want to be in on this one, so the world news will give them recognition. I'd like for you to take the Seventh Fleet to Easter Island, just to observe and assist the dredging operations in any way they need. Kartalov needs to know that we intend to keep our leadership role in this thing. The CIA pegs him as a moderate; he doesn't have much use for the Kremlin. Meet with him and kinda see where he's coming from. We could use him as a friendly contact in Moscow in the future."

"Yes, sir; I can handle that. The Seventh sailed out of San Diego yesterday. The **Neil Armstrong** is the flag ship. I'll send them new orders and have my boys fly me out there in a couple of days. I've met Leonoid a couple of times. He and I should be able to get along. I'll keep you posted, sir."

Galveston Texas - Gulf of Mexico

Steven Holmes, NASA, and Walter Brigman, US Navy, sat in the offices of Undersea Dredging and Salvage Services, waiting for the boss, Carl Weston. He was in his private office on the phone, trying to get an extension on an obligation. He had one of those voices that carries through walls and doors. Apparently successful, he hung up the phone and responded to his secretary's summons that two men were here to see him and they looked important.

He came through the door, sat down at the desk, and looked from one face to the other. "Gentlemen," he said, reaching across the desk to shake their hands, "what can I do for you?"

Walter Brigman cleared his throat. "The US Navy has discovered 50 ships around Easter Island, buried under the seabed 4000 feet below the surface of the ocean. The ships are 600 feet under the ocean floor, under the coral. We want you to dig them out."

Carl looked from face to face and then focused on Walter. "What kind of ships are they?"

"Spaceships," Walter said. "We believe they are the ships that belonged to the giants that we thought had fled into space."

"Ahhh, so they didn't take off."

"It seems that they parked there instead of fleeing into the cosmos."

"Under 4000 feet of water?"

"Yes."

Carl paused a moment. "I've got two ships that can work at that depth, however, the mandibles will have to be changed to do dredging work. Also, we will need four buoyant undersea trailers to move the material, as we dredge it, from the location."

"We'll deposit one million dollars up front with you to cover your start-up expenses and move all your equipment to Easter Island. The President wants to move right along with this. How soon can you be ready to begin?"

"Ah, very quickly," Carl responded. "In two weeks, we'll be ready to move everything there."

"Also, Mr. Weston," the Navy representative said, while filling out a blanket purchase order for Undersea Dredging and Salvage Services, "be advised, we are soliciting deep sea equipment out of Mumbai, Sidney, Southampton and Moscow as well."

"Wow, the Russians, too."

"Walter smiled, nodded, and handed Carl the Purchase Order. "The Navy will deposit the funds in your account within the week."

"I'll get you a blank check for the number."

"We have it."

Carl paused just briefly. "I must have checked out."

Walter Brigman smiled again, and nodded again. "The coral that has to be removed is from the base of the island to a quarter-mile out to sea, 600 feet deep, and circles the entire island."

"Good Lord, that will take forever!"

"We estimate two to three years."

"That sounds about right," Carl said as he escorted the two men to the door. They shook hands again, and then left.

He turned to his secretary: "Sometimes, God smiles. You want a raise?"

"Uh huh."

Carl went back into his private office to call that number back and get some more money. After a half-hour discussion, he gave the bank a PO number ending in **USN** and got another $25,000 deposited into his checking account. He would begin preparations immediately.

DAN HOLT & MAX HOLT

Chapter 3

The Astronauts

When Colonel Jimmy Austin, US Air Force, joined the Astronaut Corps, the starship Cosmos had begun to take shape. So, he adamantly sought the council of the original crew of Research One. At every opportunity, he sought interviews and spent time interacting with each member of that intrepid crew.

He had relived the saga of the discovery of the giants on the moon, and their subsequent struggle to get home, discussing it six times; five with the surviving members of Research One's crew and once with the rescued astronaut, Roger Stahls.

Colonel Stahls had run for Congress and won a seat. He chaired a committee on space regulations and appropriations. Jimmy was awed by Stahls' courage, that resulted in saving his life after having been marooned on the moon. He had put himself in suspended animation with the giants' equipment, on blind faith and sheer desperation, and had won.

Colonel Austin had read everything he could find concerning the giants of Alpha Centauri. He wanted to go there. His spirit burned to someday step out of a spacecraft onto the soil of Zannia and look across the horizon at the two suns. He wanted to see the giants, and talk to them; maybe even Mentar. And now, thanks to a wonderful occurrence, the discovery at

Easter Island, he was going to get to see a live, *hopefully live*, giant for himself. He had often tried to imagine what it would be like to climb the stairs to that specially-designed giant-size conference table and actually talk to Mentar face to face.

The government had allocated, in its annual budget for NASA, funds to build another starship; the Cosmos, a duplicate of Little One, the giants' ship. Jimmy visited the construction site as often as possible, just to look and dream.

Society was slowly changing. The Rotor Pod had begun a slow spread across the planet as the principal engine for transportation. The military services had quickly seen the potential of this genius invention and were employing the technology in many areas, especially in all types of aircraft.

A civilian version had been developed with a maximum power of *1-G* acceleration. Ground transportation had remained in place for its practicality in some important areas. Some vehicles were pod-equipped for experimental purposes, to assess their safety for general use by the public. The ground-based rotor pods had the vertical component disabled. As expected, among the older population, some had found it difficult to let go of the known and familiar.

It had been almost forty years since the debut of Magnetic Inertial Propulsion. At this juncture, it was estimated that about thirty percent of the daily commuters were in the air. The young were spearheading the transformation as they came of age.

The number of saucers, and other types of air vehicles in the sky, was growing constantly. The bureaucrats were struggling with the laws to govern the above-ground mass traffic. Metropolitan areas limited rotor-pod flight to 50 mph and inter-metropolitan flight below 2000 feet, to 300 mph. Flight level regulation was done on the points of the compass; functioning avoidance systems were required.

All civilian craft were equipped with GPS locators, automatic location reporting upon a failure, and drogue chutes with auto-deploy. The chutes would set the vehicle down with the equivalent landing of an auto-rotation emergency landing of a helicopter when its engine had failed.

Colonel Austin had been to Saturn space to visit the ancient starship, now an empty hull. He was assisting in a review on whether to use the hull, with its twenty-mile-thick outer layer, as a place to store nuclear waste. The suggestion had been to use it until full, seal it off, and let the clock run out on the half-life of the offensive material. However, considering the length of the half-life of the waste materials, thousands of years, that approach would leave the *artificial moon* as a dangerous radioactive hazard, seemingly forever.

Others had suggested that it be filled, and then steered into the sun. It was finally settled that the lapetus might be saved for another use. So, an alternate operation was established to package the nuclear waste in five-ton containers and simply place them on a solar collision course.

The Colonel had been to Mars also. It was with a study group, sent to learn the extent of the population there in the heyday of the giants and to explore the prospects of terraforming the fourth planet, a prospect that was now in process. The two original cargo ships, the Maxie Gene and the Mary Lou, built to salvage the abandoned Zannia 2, were alternating as Martian habitats for the effort. The planet was being salted with oxygen-making algae and other processes. Upon many returns to Earth, the vessels had transported the stockpile of supplies, that the Elders had collected, to Earth for storage.

Mars; the planet of live-in mountains and one-third gravity.

NASA's training now entailed all the astronauts gaining familiarity with spaceship Discovery and with the requirement to qualify on its excursion craft. They had visited all the moons of the solar system, allowing science teams to take samples, do soundings, and other investigations, including determining useful bounty.

But, NASA's main focus was growing toward star travel. Planet Earth was about to reach outward into the cosmos. She already had one neighbor and friend, "*out about ankle deep in the cosmic ocean*;" as one of the great astronomers in the past had so aptly put it.

Giant City, Kansas

Colonel Jimmy Austin parked his car again in the adjacent parking lot of the construction site of the starship Cosmos. He wanted to see if they had gotten the hundred-foot-diameter port hole mounted in the topmost hull of the ship. They were working on it the last time he was here. He processed in through the Security Checkpoint and hurried across the metal floor, around a myriad of workers, to gain a visual of the top-most area. It was there; it wasn't trimmed out yet, but they had gotten it up there and mounted; an eye to the cosmos…space.

His imagination soared ahead to when he would be in transit to the Alpha Centauri system and would check the port hole to see if he could see Zannia yet, or check the positions of the two suns shining in their glory. One was brighter than the other, and closer. He couldn't…

"Is this your first time here?" came from behind him. He jerked, then turned around. A blue-eyed dishwater blonde with a lean toned body and chiseled features extended her hand. "I'm Katherine Baylor; call me Katy."

He took her hand. "Jimmy Austin. Are you an astronaut?"

"I was accepted today. I have just *got* to board this ship and fly to Alpha Centauri."

"Me, too. Want to get some lunch?"

"Are you asking me out?"

"No, no, I…ah…Yes."

"I'll buy," Katy said, smiling.

DAN HOLT & MAX HOLT

Chapter 4

The DOEs

Easter Island
Dredging Operations

During the third month of operations, Carl Weston, topside, approached the Navy representative, Walter Brigman. "We will reach the first ship in forty-eight hours. Dredging in between it and the supply ship will have to be done by the mini-submersibles, with smaller mandibles, to avoid damage to the ships and any connections that might be in place in-between the vessels."

Brigman nodded. "Not bad, you got it ready to extract in two-and-a-half months. Looks like we will make that three-month goal on the first one. We'll have the Navy VE's here in forty-eight hours. They will remove the coral right around the smaller ship and the feeder line coming from the supply ship."

Two Days Later

Carl had his salvaging ships go through the eight-hour process of surfacing. He would do some needed maintenance on them, then move to the next spot and resume operations.

The Navy's Virtual Extension submersibles, with their human counterparts on board the host vessel on the surface, went directly to the depths of the giants' ships and began the process of removing the coral from between them.

It was discovered that the smaller ships had been plumbed to the larger ships, as suspected. Apparently, the larger ships had been loaded to capacity with the 10x10x50-foot cakes of the special gas used in suspended animation on the moon. Some questioned why the cakes of gas would have been onboard the ships when the disaster happened. How did they know?

Then it was speculated that, perhaps, the ten 360-foot-diameter ships were on their way to the moon with the gas to stockpile it there as part of the ongoing project. When the disaster occurred, the giants must have diverted them to Easter Island for their plan to protect themselves and their ships from the onslaught from Solaris 4's explosion. They apparently did not know that the destruction was total. They thought help would be coming. They apparently knew that the asteroid threat would last for a long time because of the enormous amount of debris unleashed by the explosion. So, they must have positioned themselves underneath the sea, went to sleep to stop the usage of oxygen and food, and waited.

Finally, the day came that all had been waiting for. Steven Holmes, NASA, asked the anticipated question,

"So, you have the ship free of the coral on the sea floor?"

"Yes," Walter said, "However, these guys are 4600 feet under the ocean. They will have to be brought up very slowly, taking a day for them to adjust to the changing pressure, all the way to the surface. Our VE's have been able to look inside the ship through their portholes and confirm that they are not individually separated in crates, like they were on the moon. There are four of them inside this one ship. They are in their racks and their ship is the containment unit for the sleeping gas. All four will awaken at the same time; probably sometime during the eight-hour decompressing operation on the way to the surface.

The White House

"Mr. President," Admiral Waddell said, "we are ready to bring the first ship to the surface. NASA is fabricating attachments for the VE's that will cut and seal the connection supplying the gas to the giants' ship."

"Good, let's go ahead as soon as they are ready," President Mitchell sounded.

"Well, sir, these giants are the mature scientists of their culture. Their government sanctioned unrestricted DNA manipulation and research. They experimented with DNA sequencing long ago, which is how our ancestors came to be. If the giants are alive and well, they may not regard us with the same respect as did the youths, the students, we found on the moon thirty-eight years ago. They may attempt to brush us aside and resume their agenda. As far as they know, we are the helpless *little ones* that think they are gods. I would rather that they not have to find out the hard way that they cannot take over control, as they had before the disaster."

"Good point, Admiral, what are you suggesting?"

"Preparedness. Let's have our military there when we revive these giants, to be sure that things don't get out of hand. Also, I'd like two of the armed hybrid shuttles, the DOEs from the Air Force, to be there in case the giants try to restart one of their ships and take off to who knows where."

The president paused for a moment then looked up at the Admiral. "The DOEs; *Defenders of Earth;* I remember the legislation on those. I was a senator at the time. A dozen very lethal fighters. The late General Tulles of the infamous Nevada facility, with a very eloquent speech, won approval for a dozen of them from Congress. He wanted them for the sole purpose of defending Earth from an invasion, should it occur. Very remote possibility, I think, but I guess, possible.

"The general had impeccable timing. He approached Congress just after the giants were housed at their first facility in Aurora, Illinois, and were still somewhat a mystery. Back then, the twin cannons on those DOEs would put a 50-caliber exploding bullet in every square foot of a football field in thirty seconds. The finance committee, which I was on, was shown a digital account of a demonstration of one of them. It showed it approach a building about the size of a two-car garage, lock the cannons onto it, and fire a 15-second burst. When those cannons spun to a stop, that building simply was not there anymore. There was nothing but a debris field. The biggest piece I saw was about the size of a basketball. The additional laser cannon upgrades five years ago have made those things the most lethal machines on Earth.

"The high-speed smart missiles can reach Mach 10 and engage targets up to two hundred miles above the earth, well above the atmosphere. Each missile has ten separate warheads, capable of bringing down ten separate targets."

"We've never had to use them," the admiral said. "More than likely we won't need them in this situation. But, we don't know that."

"Okay, go ahead with the DOEs and put the Marines on the Island with sufficient armament that they can contain the giants should it be necessary. But, Admiral," the president added in a serious tone, "Keep it low-key. Send a small unit, unannounced, and keep them in civilian clothes until they have to be deployed. Then, exercise extreme restraint. Only fire on the giants as a last resort, and I mean, *last resort*. If we shot them down, it would have far-reaching repercussions; very far-reaching repercussions."

"I understand, sir," the admiral said. "Hopefully, everything will go smoothly. We will enlighten the giants on everything that has transpired since the destruction of Solaris 4. I have a list of the names of the giants we revived on the moon. I'm going to quote them to these giants. They should remember Mentar, Brock, Mingee, Kronos, Juno, and many others. Maybe it will resonate with them. Perhaps, once they understand all that's happened, they will adjust."

"Let's hope so. I wish Mentar was here for this."

"Me, too," the admiral said quietly.

"The message I commissioned about this situation has been beamed to him. We'll probably hear from him in nine years and see him in twelve."

"Your probably right, sir, from what I've read about him."

Chapter 5

Juan Valencia

On a back street in New Orleans

The television blared with the volume at almost full. A flurry of activity was being broadcast from a news satellite dish on Easter Island. The reporter was announcing the confirmation that there were giants inside the submerged ships. The giants' channel once again commanded a large audience. Over the noise, the squeaky door opened.

"Is that you, Trey?"

The wrapped screen door slammed shut. "Yeah, Dad, it's me."

"Look what's on TV."

Alan Brewster III, Trey, studied the TV screen for a moment, then sat down cross-legged by his father's chair.

"Yeah, I been seeing shows about the giants."

"Did you see your Grandpa's grave?"

"Yeah. Nobody was around, so I stayed a while."

Alan Brewster Jr., feeble at 50, hard of hearing, whose inherent good looks had made him a punching bag during his tenure in federal prison, glanced at his son. He had put many of his fellow inmates in the prison hospital, but, the numbers had finally overwhelmed him and his prison life was a difficult time.

43

"Trey, go bring you daddy another beer; then I want to tell you a story."

The boy retrieved a beer from the refrigerator, popped the top and handed it to the 50-year-old, who looked more like 70, and then sat in the nearby rocker. The sweat was pouring off the old man; air conditioner hadn't worked since last year. Besides, he couldn't afford the extra electricity. Out of prison and unable to get a job, he was barely making ends meet. He took a sip of the cold brew and looked at the nine-year-old.

"Your grandfather was an astronaut."

"What?!" Trey hopped out of the rocker and sat down cross-legged in from of his father and looked up into his face. The nine-year-old's face was glowing.

Trey's reaction triggered the return of the special feelings Jr. had experienced during his vigil to disrupt the government's efforts to recover the giants from their induced sleep on the moon and bring them to Earth.

"An astronaut," Jr. repeated, smiling momentarily. "He and that fellow, Stahls, flew to the moon on a secret mission for the government. They found the giants first."

"I didn't know that!"

"Yep," Jr. continued. What little life-energy left in Alan Brewster Jr. flowed into his soul. He was now on the edge of his chair. "When your grandpa and Stahls found the giants on the moon, Stahls told you grandpa that he was going to tell everybody when they got back to Earth. Your grandfather explained to Stahls that he could not do that. It was a government secret. You can't just tell everybody government secrets.

"Dad said that Stahls was bone-headed and wouldn't listen. Your grandfather made the only decision he could make. He left Stahls there so he couldn't tell anybody."

Trey frowned. "They taught us at school that the astronaut, Roger Stahls, that went to the moon is now in Congress."

"Yeah, he is. That's what drove your grandfather crazy. He had solved the problem with Stahls and then those people that built that first flying saucer went and got him and brought him back to Earth. It drove Dad crazy and he killed himself. That's what made me blow up one of them ships. I was hoping that if would blow up on the moon. They tested it at high power and it blew up the first time they flew it.

"They found out that it was me that took those bolts out of that rotor pod and they gave me twenty years in prison. I got out in eighteen. That's when I met your mother, Juanita Valencia. Beautiful woman. She understood me. She hated cops and was really mad that they had put me in prison for so long."

"I hate cops," the boy said with a passion.

Alan Brewster Jr. reached over and touched his son on the head. "Not long after you were born, they come and got your mother and took her back to Mexico. She would be so proud of you for naming yourself after her and then going after those who messed up our family. I'm going to live as long as I can, and watch. We'll file the papers tomorrow. From now on you are going to be Juan Valencia.

Chapter 6

The Awakening

Karen Hastings, 82, and Jean Henson, 83, parked their car in front of the Chicago Linguistics Institute and entered the building.

"Karen! Jean!" Natalie Clayton, the late Della Clayton's daughter, exclaimed, "the show is on again!"

"I envy you." Karen said.

"Me, too," Jean agreed.

"We want you to be a part of this as much as you can," Natalie said enthusiastically. This is different. These are the mature ones, not students. A smile may not do it this time."

Jean laughed and her eyes moistened as the memories flowed through her mind. Karen glanced at Jean and smiled then looked back at Natalie. "Do you have anything at all, yet?"

"No," Natalie said. "They haven't brought the first ship to the surface yet and the code people haven't figured out the intercepted signal."

"Oh, by the way," Natalie said, "did I say it's good to see you again. Welcome back to the Institute. Please darken our doorway often."

"Thank you, Natalie. Soon, very soon, you are going to be busy. Just remember, these giants are the architects of all the languages we dealt with. They have very powerful computers that they ordered to create these several different languages as they genetically created these different peoples. They may even be able to speak all these languages."

Marsha Phillips, a colleague of Natalie's, joined in: "I'm a little worried about their attitude. They may assume that we are of no consequence because we are the *little ones.*"

"They will find out differently rather quickly," Jean said, "if they take that position. The Navy will take precautions for such a situation."

"Changing the subject," Natalie said, "how's Doug and Dave."

"They're fine; still active. They are working with the Navy's code people on the signals that were intercepted. They think it's a sophisticated SOS."

Karen and Jean visited with the team at the Institute for some time, then excused themselves and left with a promise to return often, especially when the Linguistics Institute began working with the mature giants of Solaris 4.

Easter Island

"Sir," the Captain of the Goliath said, "the VE's have finished the lifting cradle on the first ship. We are moving the Goliath into position to lift her to the surface. As soon as we are linked up you can have your people sever the gas supply line and seal it off, in about an hour."

When the Goliath was ready to begin the transfer to the surface of the first ship, one of the VE's was steered to a porthole of the vessel and stationed there for a visual of the interior. The ship would be lifted in eight segments, with a one-hour pause at each level, until reaching the surface. The vigil began at 6:00 a.m. At 2:30 p.m. the ship was sitting on the shore of Easter Island, with water still dripping from her circular rim. The tripod gear was down and seemed undamaged. The Admiral ordered the Marines at the ready. The commander stationed twelve near the ship and twelve in reserve. If they were forced to fire upon them, they were ordered to wound only.

"Okay," Admiral Waddell said, "go ahead and remove our seal from the feeder line."

Two technicians removed the sealing plug from the severed tube. There was a brief equalization of pressure to the surrounding atmosphere and a small amount of sea water dripped form the end of the tube. The residual gas in the ship lasted longer than anticipated.

"Anything yet?" Admiral Waddell said.

"No, sir," Walter Brigman responded. They haven't moved yet. This ship held a considerable volume of the gas."

The giants slept on for almost an hour. The Admiral had begun to consider gaining entrance to the vessel to see if there was indeed a problem; that perhaps they had not survived but had been preserved. Then the alarm was voiced: "One of them moved!

The younger of the four giants inside the first ship raised his head up, looked around at the ship, then at the porthole. He saw the VE recording the interior of the ship. He stared at it momentarily, then dropped his head back down on his rack and rubbed his face. He raised his head again, then sat up on the side of his rack and studied the porthole. He got to his feet, stepped to the next rack and shook his colleague.

The second giant stirred, sat up, and looked up at his crewmate. He pointed at the porthole. They both stood, stepped over to it, and studied the piece of machinery that had affixed itself to the transparent window. They spoke briefly, then began looking out the porthole around the VE. They spotted the *little ones* standing around outside, including the twelve Marines in the background, lined up in an orderly fashion, all dressed in like garb.

They immediately awakened the other two crewmembers of the alien craft. Minutes later the four-man crew was awake and listening to a discourse from the first one to awaken, glancing at the porthole and outside.

A full thirty minutes later, an elderly-appearing giant pointed at the door of the spacecraft. The first one to awaken stepped over to it and activated a control. The door of the craft slid to the side and a ramp extended from the perimeter to the ground. The older crewmate stepped out onto the hull of the ship, looked around, and then spoke in Moon.

Admiral Waddell responded in English: "We do not understand what you are saying."

When the giant heard English being spoken, he stepped back and pointed at another member of his crew and motioned for him to come forward. The younger-appearing giant came out onto the hull of the ship and addressed the Admiral in perfect English: "Where are your custodians?"

"Custodians?" Admiral Waddell repeated. "What does that mean?"

Walter spoke up: "Admiral, he wants to know where the giants are that have custody of you."

Admiral Waddell pulled a list of names out of his inside coat pocket and then looked up at the giant. "You're name, sir?"

The giant looked around at his crewmates, with the stirrings of a smile on his lips, spoke briefly in Moon, and then turned back to the Admiral. "Kavientar Kaavienne."

"I'm Admiral Waddell. Apparently, you are not aware of how long you have been sleeping. I'm sorry to say that all the, so called, custodians perished in the ancient disaster. We were shielded in caves at that time and managed to survive."

Kaveintar turned to his crew and began a rapid discourse in Moon that lasted several minutes. Momentarily, he rejoined the conversation. "How long have we been waiting," he said, gesturing toward the ocean depths.

Admiral Waddell spoke slowly: "Fifty thousand years."

Kavientar reacted so profoundly that the Admiral paused and waited for a moment before resuming: "The debris from Solaris 4, over time, destroyed life on all the planets in the Solar System except Earth. Your people, heroically, put the students who were working and training on the moon safely underground in suspended animation, as you yourselves did here. We, at the time of the disaster, were in caves, as I said, here on Earth and survived as well.

"Now, fifty thousand years later, we have grown to the beginnings of space flight and while exploring the moon, we found the students along with their counselors, Mentar, Brock, Mingee, and Meta Kaavienne. Twelve hundred and twelve students and the four counselors survived. We revived them from their extended sleep and brought them to Earth almost forty years ago. We made the arrangements and they built a city with the appropriate dimensions for themselves to live in here on Earth."

Kavientar quickly turned to the crew and spoke rapidly again in Moon for a minute then turned back to the Admiral. "Where are they?"

"They went home to Zannia years ago"

"How?"

Admiral Waddell paused a long moment. "Kavientar, there's much that has happened since you went to sleep. We have linguists that will be working with you and your people and will bring you up to date. First we must tend to the business at hand—getting the rest of your people topside to safety."

Kavientar nodded. "What happened to the Moon Laboratory where you found our students?"

"The debris from Solaris 4 ruptured the Arcology and it was opened to the vacuum of space. All who were not in the animation units perished."

The giant relayed the information to his colleagues. Two of them immediately looked up at the sky, found the faint lunar disc, and stared at it momentarily. The eyes of the rest followed.

Walter glanced up at the moon. He experienced a moment of sadness for them. They had been completely removed from their elite status. The horrendous mistake by their research people had far-reaching effects on their culture.

The spokesman again focused on the Admiral. "How many of us made it through the sleep?"

"We don't know yet. You are the first to be brought topside. Your ships, over time, were slowly encased in the ocean coral, six hundred feet of it, and it has to be removed. It will take two to three years to get all your vessels out of the sea and your people revived. We will take you to the city built by Mentar and the students while they were here. We have brought in a temporary dwelling for you and your crew here on the island, until all your survivors are topside."

"How did you know that we would be alive?"

"We didn't. Had your animation system failed, the temporary dwelling would have been your morgue. Fortunately, fate smiled on you."

Kavientar was silent for a moment, then nodded.

The admiral continued: "We will need you here to orient the remaining crews about what has happened as we bring them to the surface. Hopefully, they have all survived. How many of you were there when you entered the ocean depth's?"

"Two hundred," Kavientar responded. "How many are there of you?"

Admiral Waddell paused a moment, looked around at the four giants, then focused back on their spokesman: "Counting all colors, all across the planet, just over seven billion."

Kavientar was visibly shaken. He related the answer to the rest of the crew. A strange quiet settled on the giants for several moments. "You have become a civilization," Kavientar said.

"Mentar will be coming to take you home; your original home. While we wait for his arrival, there's much we can learn from each other. Let's get the rest of your people topside and then to Mentar's City."

Chapter 7

The Lunar Excursion

Mentar City, Kansas

Dwight Cummins, 62, was reactivated as liaison to the giants. This time he had more service to offer. He now spoke fluent Moon, the native tongue of the giants. No one knew what the native language of the giants was called, not even the giants themselves. All members of their species spoke the same language—it just was. The language was designated as *Moon* by the human *little ones* because the first giants known were discovered on the moon.

Once again, Dwight had an opportunity to serve his country in his most cherished job. In his last tenure of service, he had been in the position to be the first one to know about the first pregnancy among the giants when they occupied Giant City, now Mentar City, Kansas. He'd never forgotten those defining moments. Now, he would have the adventure of getting to know the fathers and mothers of the students that had been here before. What an odd reversal. He parked his personal saucer at the edge of town, stepped out, patted the seal of the Diplomatic Corp on the side, and began his stroll through Mentar City.

Workmen were everywhere removing the tourist advertisements and booths. Colorful banners were being taken down. It was amazing how many entrepreneurial pursuits had crept into the city, built by and for the giants, after Mentar and company had left for home. The vacationing public had a hunger for everything giant, making the souvenir business very good. Thousands of replicas of the giants' everyday tools; forks, spoons, toothbrushes, combs, pencils, and many other everyday items had been sold from Giant City, Kansas. Now, Giant City would be freshened as Mentar City. The giants would live here again.

Dwight, finishing his tour, entered his personal vehicle and headed back to Washington to report. It was good, very good.

Easter Island

The first crew of giants that were brought to the surface were introduced to the temporary tent dwelling the U.S. Navy had installed. The military arranged for the Army Quartermaster Corps to deliver food and clothing. Their chefs began providing food.

The four giants, now topside, looked around at the large tent and its associated appointments. The Navy flew in two linguists from the Chicago Linguistics Institute, both fluent in Moon, to confer with the giants at length on the present status of the Solar System and their world, as it was. Along with the linguists, fluent in Moon, the aging crew that had worked with the giants upon their discovery, Doug and Karen Hastings and Dave and Jean Henson accompanied them for a few days, to confer with the newly awakened giants, the Elders, to help them understand the current *giant/little one* relationship. A world lost and a new one found.

"Sir," Walter Brigman said to the Admiral, "I had just entered the Navy when Mentar and the students were here. These giants are different; they seem distant."

"I've noticed that. It is well to note, however, that they won't be as moldable as the young students were. These people had their lifeways, priorities, and habits, and now, all that has been ripped away."

"It makes me a little uneasy," Walter said.

"Everyone involved in their recovery has been briefed. Hopefully, they will come around in time. They are lucky that we found them. They were already in their graves had we not picked up their SOS. I think they know that."

The sun touched its yellow orb to the waters of the vast ocean around Easter Island. The shadows of the Moai reached far inland. Darkness crept across the island. Two sentries were posted in the complex consisting of a tent city accommodating the teams of undersea specialists, the headquarters tent, the modified circus tent, several aircraft housing twenty-four Marines and their equipment, the giant's recovered spacecraft, and the two DOEs. The DOEs were piloted by Captain Snyder, the ranking officer, and Captain Abbott. The two crews of the fighters, a pilot, copilot, navigator, and gunner, used their ships as billeting; thereby always ready to respond if needed.

10:00 pm

Quiet gripped the island. The only sound was the repetitious lapping of the ocean waves against the shore and the whisper of a gentle breeze flowing through the complex. The two guards sat on some rocks near the shore, talking idly between themselves. One of them suddenly straightened up. "Did you hear that?"

"What?"

"I thought I heard something; it was a bumping sound."

"I didn't hear anything."

The sentry listened intently for a moment. "Maybe it was the wind."

The guards resumed small talk, trying to say alert under the relentless lullaby of the ocean waves. Minutes later, a whirring sound found their ears. They looked at each other and then jumped to their feet and ran into the camp. The giants' ship was powering up. The hatch was closed and the ramp had been retracted.

The sentry grabbed his radio. "Captain Snyder! Captain Snyder! The giants are powering up their ship!" Seconds later, the sentry saw the lights come on in the cabins of the fighters and heard the powerful rotor pods starting up.

The other sentry ran to the headquarters tent and burst inside, waking the Admiral and his assistant. "Sir," he shouted, "the giants are powering up their ship!"

Walter jumped off his cot, bolted out the door, and ran to the circus tent of the giants. Two of them were still there. They were sleeping soundly. He shook the English-speaking giant several times. He finally began to stir, then opened his eyes and rubbed his face.

"Who are the two members of your crew that are powering up your ship!" Walter shouted.

Kavientar sat up, rubbed his face again, then looked around the tent. He spotted the two empty cots. He stared at them momentarily. "Kaagan and Letar; it's Kaagan and Letar."

Admiral Waddell hurried out the tent just in time to see the giants' ship leave the ground. The ship's lights were brilliant and oscillating around the perimeter of the vessel. The DOEs rose rapidly from the ground and matched the ascent of the alien craft. Admiral Waddell grabbed the sentry's radio. "DOEs, this is Admiral Waddell, do not fire on them, repeat, do not fire on them. Stay with them and see where they are going."

"Yes, sir, understood; negative fire," was the response from both fighters.

"Keep us informed."

"Yes, sir."

The Admiral hurried to the giant's tent. The two remaining giants were sitting up on their cots. The English-speaking Kavientar was conversing with Walter Brigman. Walter had just inquired: "Where are they going?"

Kavientar conferred with his crewmate for a few moments then turned to Walter. "Both of them had children serving with the students on the moon when the explosion occurred. Kaagan and Letar were working on programming on Solaris 3…ah…Mars. By the time they had gotten back to the moon it had already been destroyed and the bombardment was still going on. We flew directly here to protect ourselves from the same fate. No doubt, Kaagan and Letar are on their way to the moon."

Admiral Waddell borrowed the radio again. "DOEs, come in."

"Go ahead, sir."

"We believe the giants are on their way to the moon. Can you stay with them?"

"Sir, we could fly circles around them. So far their greatest acceleration has been less than *one-half G*."

"I mean are you prepared for that long a flight."

"Oh, yes, sir. These DOEs are kept stocked with thirty day's provisions."

"Good. Don't let the giants out of your sight. Keep us informed."

"Yes, sir."

In Lunar Trajectory

The trio of ships sailed on into the night. The brilliant full moon peeped around the giants' ship at the two fighters pacing it some 300 yards astern. Captain Snyder, DOE 1, glanced at his speed readout. The giants were cruising at *point-four-six G*. He wondered if that was the ship's power limit or was it a deliberate setting. He looked over at his double, DOE 2. He was unable to see Captain Abbott in the dim glow of the cockpit. He keyed his ship to ship: "Abbott."

"Yeah."

"How's everything over there?"

"We're good. Two of my crew are trying to get a little more sleep. How about you?"

"We're okay," Snyder replied. Wonder why these giants headed for the moon?"

"Maybe their parents were there or perhaps their children and they want to know one way or another."

"I would."

"Yeah, me, too."

3:00 am
Approaching mid-point reverse of power

Snyder keyed his radio; "Island Security, come in, please."

"Go ahead."

"Is the Admiral asleep?"

"Yes, yes he is."

"Okay. This is a routine report. Please inform the Admiral when he awakens. The time is 3:00 a.m. and the giants are still on trajectory to the moon, cruising at *point-four-six G*. Mid-point is coming up in twenty-one minutes. Transit time at this velocity is almost eleven hours. We'll be arriving at about 9:00 a.m. your time. Will contact you upon arrival. Please inform the Admiral the moment he's awake."

"Will do."

The giants' ship came to a stop one hundred and forty miles above the moon. Captain Snyder informed Admiral Waddell of their arrival and received instructions to stay with them and continue the reports.

Momentarily, the giant's ship hovered, seemly unconcerned about their fighter escorts, and then began a descent to the lunar surface. The giants descended into the ancient central crater, paused, and then slowly circled the landing marks imprinted on the surface of the mold, where the huge glass panes had been made to build the protective dome for the city. Many travelers, that passed this way to *touch and go*, had been leaving those marks. The two giants then headed for the huge complex. As they approached, they spotted and set a course for the dominate crater that had opened the door to the underground tunnel. The ship, followed by the two DOE fighters, descended into the crater to the tunnel opening. It hovered for several moments as the giants examined a, now empty, tunnel. The many glass crates had been taken to Earth and put in storage. Captain Benjamin Snyder was reporting a continuing commentary to the Admiral as the mystery unfolded.

Soon, the giants' vessel rose out of the crater and flew the length of the complex. It continued slowly above the apex of the glass mountain until it reached the opposite end, some twenty miles. It paused momentarily, then continued until it overflew the vast gas storage area. It paused there for a few moments and then returned to the complex and the open access on the North end. The ship entered the open shaft and began the long descent straight down into the complex. The two escorts followed, noting in their report that they may be out of radio contact for some time.

Captain Snyder turned and glanced at his crew. "Clancy, you and Stevens, suit up."

"Yes, sir," Clancy responded. The two crewmembers got into their pressure suits, minus the helmets.

"Sir," Stevens said, "weapons?"

The Captain paused only seconds. "Negative. If they are going where I think they're going, I will highlight the Dedication Marker with the ship's lighting and you gentlemen will exit the ship, come to attention, and salute the fallen."

The giants, descending the vertical shaft, noticed a missing door from one of the bays. The lights came on in the giant's vessel. Spontaneously, the two DOEs' lights came on. Then, just below the open door, the giants spotted a damaged wall where, many years earlier, one of the guppies had crashed into it. They paused their ship momentarily, then continued until they reached the bottom of the shaft. They noted the shattered door that had fallen over a mile to crash into the floor. Then they turned toward the lab and proceeded onward. The DOEs followed at a discreet distance. The giants exited the tunnel into the, now near-empty, lab. The ships' lighting revealed an eerie, abandoned, tomb of death. When the DOEs exited the tunnel into the lab behind them, the added lighting revealed many left-behind fixtures in faint silhouettes. The giants paused only briefly, then proceeded on to the tunnel that extended to the end of the complex. Ahead, they could see their destination. When the tunnel began to narrow, they descended to the floor and parked their ship at the hallway opening to the lower crypt.

"Okay," the captain said, "that's where they're going. Put on your helmets and enter the air lock and depressurize."

Half an hour later the two giants exited their ship in pressure suits and proceeded down the hallway toward the lower tunnel.

"Captain Abbott, standby here with their ship. I'll follow them in."

"Yes, sir."

The giants quickly stepped over to the wall switching-system, barely visible in the dim lighting of their ship parked sixty feet away, and turned on the lights. They walked briskly down the access hallway and entered the tunnel where the 400 students and their two Counselors were entombed. They walked right around the dedication marker and went straight to the first crate and looked inside. They both showed a visible reaction and looked at each other. They moved to the next crate, viewed the remains, and then to the next.

Captain Snyder rotated his ship to focus his lights brightly on the dedication pillar, then touched down and opened the outer doors. Kaagan and Letar noticed the movement of the DOE, so they straightened up and watched. Clancy and Stevens marched down the ramp in lock-step, out ten feet from the ship, faced the marker, and rendered a salute, holding it for one minute.

The two giants, watching them, looked at each other, then slowly walked over to the marker, and read the caption etched on top in *Moon.* They looked at each other again and quickly went down on one knee and began reading the names. It took them several minutes to scan all 400 etchings on the dedication pillar. When the first giant finished reading the last name, he jumped up, briefly leaving the stone floor in the low gravity, then raised both arms straight over his head, smiling broadly. His partner did the same.

"Apparently, the names of their children were not there," Snyder said. "That means that they are still alive and living on Zannia."

The two giants, after a few minutes, became calm and solemn. They turned back to the sea of glass crates sitting quiet and still as they had for many centuries. Momentarily, they looked at the marker again and reread the caption on top. Each laid a hand on it, and then they headed back to their ship.

Snyder reversed his ship, back into the entrance hallway and keyed his ship-to-ship radio.

"Abbott, they're coming out."

Captain Abbott responded: "Standing by."

The two giants entered their ship. Minutes later, it lifted off and proceeded out the end of the tunnel, into the impact crater and then upward. The ship had set course toward the east. The damaged castle-looking structure, hanging from the overhead rigging some thirty miles above the lunar surface, loomed in the distance.

Captain Snyder raised the Admiral on Earth and filled him in on the giants visit to the underground lab and the entombed students and the results.

"Good move, Captain," came from the Admiral.

"Sir, it appears that the giants have now set course for the Castle. We are following them."

"Roger, Captain, standing by here."

The giants proceeded on course for the Castle. In route, from time to time, they slowed their vessel to view certain areas of the devastation below, then would resume. Finally, upon arrival at the Castle, they ascended to the top of the building and flew around the suspended structure. They then paused at the hundred-foot square opening where the pane of glass had fallen out of the wall and smashed into the foundation of the ancient building far below. They paused momentarily then ascended to two floors above the opening, to where the building reduced in size. Their ship hovered. Minutes later the ramp opened and came to rest on the ledge of the building. One of the giants, still in his pressure suit, stepped out of the vessel onto the ledge, walked over to the wall of the structure, grasped the handle of an outside door and slid it to the side. He entered the building and disappeared.

The giant was inside the structure for some ten minutes, then he reappeared carrying a container, four-by-six feet and two-feet deep. It appeared to be metal. The giants re-entered their ship, closed the outer door and retracted the ramp. They headed back to the central crater. Upon arrival, they immediately ascended to one-hundred-forty miles, then paused. Shortly afterward, their ship launched at *point-four-six-G*, headed for Earth. Captain Snyder apprised the Admiral and the two fighters followed.

Admiral Waddell informed Kavientar of his colleague's investigation of the lab and the tunnels on the moon. He then outlined their flight to the main building of the Arcology, the so-called, castle and the container they retrieved from that structure.

"Records," Kavientar responded, "that building housed all the records for the Retirement Center on the moon. The names of everyone there are recorded. It was updated daily. Every arrival and every departure."

The Admiral's personal phone signaled an incoming call from the fighters. He hurried to his office. "Go ahead, Captain."

"I thought you would want to know, sir. The giants approached Earth over southern Canada. They have turned Southwest and are on a course to overfly the great lakes, Chicago, and if they continue on this course, they will pass over Wichita and Mentar City, Kansas. They will see Cosmos under construction. The site is always ablaze with lights."

"Did the approach seem to be planned?"

"Not really, sir. There was no major course correction."

"Very well. They'll be here soon then."

"They are averaging about 500 miles per hour."

"About six or seven hours. Thank you, Captain."

The DOE's continued to pace the giants' ship, well astern. When the ship entered Chicago air space, two security craft rose up from the city's airport to check out the unregistered vessel. When they spotted the DOEs following the ship, they waved, then broke off and returned to the city.

When the giants reached Wichita, Kansas, they spotted the well-lighted construction site of Cosmos and the adjacent Mentar City. They slowed and circled the two sites three times, then resumed south over the gulf, across Mexico, and out to sea.

The two giants, Kaagan and Letar, approached Easter Island just as the sun peeped over the horizon, pushing away the darkness. They touched down in the same spot where Goliath had deposited the spacecraft upon lifting it from the ocean depths. The door opened and they came down the ramp carrying the records storage container. They carried it into the tent just as if it was a prearranged task.

Admiral Waddell watched them from the time they left the door of their ship until they disappeared into the tent. "They assume that they have carte blanche."

Walter, watching the giants as well, glanced at the Admiral. "I doubt if they've ever known anything else. In their world, they were the biggest and smartest."

"Do you think they understand that that world is no more?"

"Admiral, they're not stupid. They just don't know how to act. If I may say so, sir, you're handling of this situation has been exemplary. Consider their plight and cut them some slack."

Irwin Waddell paused a moment then looked at Walter and nodded.

Captains Snyder and Abbott landed their DOEs back in their respective places and reported to the Admiral. Admiral Waddell returned their salute. "Gentlemen, good job."

"Thank you, sir."

The Admiral measured his words: "We are sailing in uncharted territory here. These two giants, meaning no harm, simply went to check on their children by stealth; without showing us the courtesy of informing us. That shows how poor our understanding of each other really is and, perhaps, how little they regard us. I wanted to alert you that, as we bring all these giants up from the ocean, we may encounter some that are upset, maybe even hostile, about what's happened to them. If we encounter a bad apple, or a group of malcontents, and they endanger our people here, fire a warning volley over their heads. They should come to their senses. If not, the marines are instructed to wound only."

"Understood, sir."

"However, don't allow our people to come to harm. You are authorized to take them down if you have too."

"Yes, sir."

Captains Snyder and Abbott, with their crews, returned to their DOEs and crawled into their racks to sleep the sleep of a soldier.

Chapter 8

Out of the Depths

Kavientar was glued to the deep-sea monitor, watching the second ship in his circle being prepared for extraction from the sea. When the images of the crew inside the ship appeared, he leaned over for a closer look. He then turned to Kaagan. "Five; there are five on board. The crew is only four...why are there five?"

Kaagan looked closely. The fifth occupant of the ship was a young giant; more of a teenager. "Oh, yes, I remember. That's Menvaar Ataar Kaavienne. You were already in the cockpit, preparing for our supply mission to the moon when this youngster came into the Departure Port. The Elders had approved his last-minute request to accompany the fleet to the moon, for a surprise visit with his father, who had been assigned there to work with the Retirement Center trainees. Our second ship had the extra seat, so he joined them. His father will be extremely pleased to learn that he survived."

Kavientar turned. "His father survived? Who is his father?"

"Mentar, the Counselor."

Upon hearing the news, the President had NASA immediately send another message, addressed

71

specifically to Mentar. Menvaar would be over four years older before his father even knew he was alive.

The days turned into weeks and the weeks were approaching three months. The Admiral had a Virtual Extension Monitor set up in the temporary dwelling of the giants so they could monitor the operation. The remaining three ships of the first group were brought topside. While the VEs were dredging the final coral free of the first cargo ship, the Monolith, another heavy lift ship, was brought in the assist with the larger vessel. The 360-foot diameter craft, still loaded with a remaining twenty-five percent of its capacity of the wax cakes, was deposited on dry land by the Goliath and Monolith.

A giant cavern in the Colorado mountains, prepared years earlier to deal with the lunar and Martian discoveries, was used to store the remaining gas removed from the supply ship. The giant population on Easter Island grew as the dredging operation continued. Each of the awakened crews was oriented by their own and were thoroughly informed of their present status by the linguists assigned to the recovery process. When the population of the giants' tent approached capacity, twenty-five at a time were escorted to Mentar City to take up residence there for the foreseeable future; that is, until Mentar arrived to take them home.

The Easter Island Project had taken on the atmosphere of routine as the groups of linked ships were separated by the VEs and brought to the surface. The giant crews were allowed an awakening time, then oriented to their *back to life in a new world*, reality.

The dredging and clearing process continued to be routine until the VEs began their clearing of group number seven. When the sensitive Virtual Extension unit began clearing the coral from around the gas supply line to the first of the four receiving ships, a section of the one-foot diameter pipe broke loose and slowly settled to the ocean floor below. The Virtual Extension pilot paused his undersea equipment, looked at the digital image again, then turned to his assistant. "Go get the Admiral."

Admiral Waddell stared at the image on the pilot's monitor for a long moment, then, knowing what it meant, looked at the floor in silence. Momentarily, he looked up at the VE pilot. "This is on the giants' monitor inside their tent?"

"Yes, sir."

"Standby." The admiral and his assistant left the pilot's station and went directly to the giants' tent and entered. The giants had gathered around the screen and were talking quietly in Moon. They paused and looked around when they became aware of the Admiral's presence.

He told them, "I'll have the pilot steer the VE into position to take a look inside the ships."

The English-speaking giant repeated the notice to his colleagues, then turned to the Admiral and nodded solemnly. "Okay."

Admiral Waddell nodded to his assistant who hurried back to the control cubicle of the VE. Momentarily the image on the monitor moved slowly to the porthole of the entombed vessel, and then contacted it. A powerful light came on and the inside of the ship was illuminated. The giants, glued to the monitor, all reacted with an obvious sadness for the loss of their colleagues. The image on the monitor revealed that the crew had perished long ago and the undersea life had taken their natural course with the remains. The ship was half full of sea water. The VE operator solemnly checked the other ships in the network. They were all the same. The total loss of life to the giants was twenty members. The VE retreated and went on standby.

The Admiral paused for a few moments, then spoke to Kavientar: "Apparently, a meteor strike nearby rippled the undersea ocean floor near these ships and severed that feeder line. I will move the crews to the next network of ships. I know this is not a matter for a snap decision but perhaps you and your colleagues would want to consider two plans to appropriately handle this. One; bring them up and intern them at Mentar City to be remembered, or, two, leave them there, in their ships, and position the Moai on the shore looking out over their resting place with an appropriate dedication marker."

Kavientar looked down on the Admiral's upturned face for a long, searching, moment, then around at his colleagues whose faces showed question. He then looked back to the Admiral and nodded solemnly, before turning back to his colleagues and speaking in Moon.

The line-of-sight-highway
Earth to Alpha Centauri

The digital message, traveling at 186,000 miles per second, the speed of light, continued on toward the powerful receiving and transmitting equipment on Peak Island, Zannia, four-and-a-half light-years from Earth. The message was approaching the half-way point. Thirteen and a half trillion miles left to go. Upon arrival it would be a call to Mentar from some friends.

Giant City, Kansas

Kavientar and his crew, in their ship, were escorted to Mentar City to meet with the other survivors of the elders regarding the development at Easter Island. Upon arrival, they were given a general tour of the metropolis, before the meeting began. The special design of the conference table allowed the president's liaison, Dwight Cummins, to monitor and keep the president informed.

Dwight sat quietly during the meetings and conferences in which the giants were all given a voice in determining the disposition of the issue at Easter Island. Dwight became aware, quite by surprise, that underneath the arrogant demeanor of these scientists, engineers, and technical-types from Solaris 4, there was heart. They did not handle that conflicting behavior very well, but it was there and it was real. They had never been questioned, opposed, contested, or called into account for their choice of values and lifeways since the *great separation* of their civilization many centuries earlier.

In Dwight's vigil of learning to speak Moon, he had read about the ancient *splitting* of their society and the spiritualists leaving and taking up residence on Venus, the tropical planet of the Solar System. The explosion of Solaris 4 had unmercifully wiped out all life on that planet. Now, the elders, the scientists, had awakened to a world where they have been completely replaced, ironically, by their own creation.

It was finally settled that the giants preferred to leave their colleagues entombed under the sea with the dedication marker in place. It seemed to them that it was fitting and respectful, as was the crypt of stone on the moon. Kaagan and Letar had related to the giants that they witnessed the respectful tribute by their escort, the *little ones*, on the moon. They had learned, at that honoring, that their offspring still lived.

Chapter 9

Mentar City

With Earth, once again, hosting a colony of giants, legislation was quickly created and passed to officially change the name of the landmark, Giant City, Kansas, to Mentar City, Earth. Worldwide media outlets had been buzzing with the news that Mentar's son had survived. The young giant was a little timid with all of the attention, especially when the American President invited him to be his special guest on the podium, as he recut the big red ribbon, renaming Giant City, Kansas to Mentar City, Earth. Menvaar felt quite awkward, holding on to the ceremonial scissors as the *little one's* president cut the ribbon. Celebrity status did not suit him well.

Menvaar remembered nothing about the 50,000 years of sleep. From his perspective, he had only left Mars a few weeks ago. He remembered the emergency alarms the fleet had received, reporting the explosion of Solaris 4 and the rapid conversations with the authorities on the moon, directing the fleet to take refuge on Earth. He had begged the pilot to continue to the moon and pick up his father. The pilot ignored his plea, saying he was much too busy, trying to save his craft from the disaster.

It seemed like yesterday to Menvaar, that the ship landed on the water near a small deserted island on Earth, and bobbed up and down, as the pilot waited orders from the commander of the fleet. He remembered his first bout with sea sickness. Soon, the fleet descended to the depths near the island and scouted appropriate places to wait, safe from the meteors beginning to rain from the sky.

Young Menvaar remembered being bored, waiting at the bottom of the ocean, separated from the other ships by water, and not really knowing the four crew crewmembers. He was afraid for himself and his father. The crew had discussions about the gravity of what had happened and made *guesses* about the condition of the moon. They wanted to be encouraging for Menvaar, but the consensus was that the moon… didn't make it.

Finally, the decision was made. The Fleet Commander had all ships on combined radio link to issue his instructions. Menvaar still remembered his words.

"Fellow pilots and crew members. We find ourselves in an emergency situation of unknown proportions. We know there has been an explosive event on Solaris 4 that has impacted all planets and moons in the Sol System. Most likely, the damage has been severe, even on the moon. Our last communication with them confirmed that they were preparing for a significant impact of debris. I just hope that some portion of the Acrology will survive.

But, being a realist, I must prepare us for the worst. Our detection devices tell us that random debris from the disaster is still impacting the earth. An inventory of ships' stores confirms that we only have provisions for 30 more days. However, we have an unlimited supply of animation gas, since our mission was to deliver vast stores of it to the Acrology on the moon.

I am directing the following actions, while we wait for rescue, which I am confident will come. First, the laser-equipped ships will surface and land on the island. I have instructed them to carve a signal from the rock surface…something that the primitive inhabitants would never understand but that our rescuers would recognize immediately as our location.

Upon their return to the depths, we will arrange all small ships around the cargo vessels carrying the cakes of animation gas. Our ships are not equipped with sleep pods, but we can use the construction supplies we are carrying to construct pipe connections to the gas cakes and use our ships as sleep pods. We must get these actions accomplished within 10 days so that we will still have provisions left for when we are rescued. I'm sure our families will be glad to see us when we finally get back to Mars."

The commander's actions having been completed, he directed each crew to prepare one last meal before the gas would be released into the ships. Menvaar remembered how he ate very little…his worry about his father had quieted his appetite. He remembered how, when the final order was given, he closed his eyes, expecting to be awakened soon.

Easter Island

Operations at Easter Island removed and recovered the final group of survivors and all were moved to Mentar City, Earth, the now-recognized outpost of Zannia. The giants' ships were parked at The Frank Gordon Space Center adjacent to Mentar City and were available to the giants for prudent use.

The giants spent some time adjusting to their new and different environment. Kavientar set up English classes for daily tutoring of the giant population. After all, they had years to spend on Earth until a starship arrived from their home, and, or, the starship under construction in the distance was finished.

The sun came and went. The newness slowly waned and the giants settled in for the duration. The universities around the country could not pass up the depository of untapped knowledge present in Mentar City. As the giants became fluent in English, multiple invites to lecture at the places of learning came to them. The most requested was Hyper-dimensional physics, the theory of gleaning energy from higher dimensions through magnetic fields. This field of study was thought the most important to be understood. Reckless experimentation with the concept had released enormous amounts of energy that had virtually destroyed the Solar System.

Additionally, many of the giant scientists, were asked to lecture on a variety of subjects: inertial force, solar-mechanical systems, metallurgy, DNA research and the like. For the giants, it seemed to be food for the soul. That's what they were; put crudely, containers of knowledge. Up until their paths crossed with the *developed little ones*, knowledge was the single marker of importance.

Now, it was different, and puzzling. Mentar, a simple counselor, had commanded great respect among his peers and was hailed as a great leader by the *little ones*. This outpost of Zannia now hailed his name.

Menvaar had always been proud of his father. Now, there had been confirmation that his civilization, what was left of it, was equally as proud. He knew these *little ones* would take some getting used to, but their honoring of Mentar would endure them to his young heart, far into the future.

DAN HOLT & MAX HOLT

Chapter 10

Kaavar, Zannia

Alpha Centauri System
Two years later

A group of signals, in transit for four-and-a-half years, entered the double-star system and washed upon the shores of a freshened planet. They contained a special message for the planet's leader, a message that would be of extreme interest.

Mentar started his day on the top floor of the Central Administration Building, a building sitting on top of a pedestal some 400 feet above the complex grounds of Zannia's capital city, Kaavar. His secretary, Maavienne, opened the curtain over the vast picture window in front of his desk. In the distance was the starship, Little One, sitting proudly in its special launching pad. Though two miles away, its bulk, a half-a-mile across and a quarter-mile high, still dominated the city skyline. A skyline that was a forest of single-pedestal-type structures with saucer-shaped buildings sitting on top of them. The pedestals held the buildings above giant trees, bushes, and shrubs, averaging roughly seven times the size of their counterparts on Earth. Mentar had ordered the layout of the Central Administration Complex so the ship would be, when moored, dead center of his viewing window. Mounted on the wall to the left of the picture window was an eight-by-twelve-foot painting and very good likeness of Colonel Marvin Dean Andrews. He had been the commander of the spaceship, Discovery, that rescued the giants from the moon. Oft times, Mentar, when faced with an important decision, would look at the painting and whisper, "What would you do, Colonel?"

When Little One arrived on Zannia, the starter civilization on board the starship found a planet in disrepair. They had circumnavigated it, locating the cities, towns, and various way-stations serving some purpose when Zannia was still livable. The Zannians had begun refurbishing the planet immediately. They had cleared an ancient spaceport and revitalized it. The millions of board-feet of materials produced went to restore a world. The Zolaadine ore mines underneath the nearby mountains had to be reactivated. They were the only source of the metal necessary to build pedestals of the strength required to support the giant buildings. The first new construction completed was the Seat of Government.

Mentar's secretary tapped on the door and then entered. "Sir, there's a courier here from Peak Island. He says it's very important."

"Send him in,"

The courier entered, approached Mentar's desk, and placed a printed copy of a digital message in front of Zannia's president. Mentar picked up the dispatch and began to read. The second line of text instructed him to view the second page of the document. He did so. Immediately he buzzed his secretary. "Call Brock, Mingee, Meta, Kronos, Juno, and Nycron and have them come to my office immediately."

Within an hour, the six government officials were in Mentar's office conference room. Mentar handed the received message to them to read and pass on. As they digested the document, Mentar saw the sparkle of adventure surface in their eyes. "Brock, Mingee, and Meta, would you like one more journey to Earth to pick up our own? I've already ordered a complete maintenance review and readiness of Little One. Kronos, you will step into the seat of government, along with Juno and Nycron, until we return."

The nods were immediate. Mentar continued: "I'm having Maavienne contact all the Zannians who were born on Earth, and their parents, informing them that Little One will be returning to their place of birth, and why. Maavienne was born on Earth and has already claimed the first seat."

"They'll all be aboard, count on it," Brock said. "They could not pass up such an opportunity."

"I know," Mentar said and was quiet for a moment, then he said, "Brock, Mingee, and Meta, there's one other thing I want to talk to you about; to you first, then involve all Zannians. In the daily feed that we receive from Earth on Peak Island, there's discourse about Earth's desire to have an outpost here on Zannia and the reciprocal on Earth, Giant City, Kansas. In effect a colony from Earth here on Zannia and a colony of Zannians on Earth."

Brock spoke up: "You're suggesting that we take a permanent colony to Earth when we go after the Elders?"

Mentar nodded. "Yes. The people of Earth are building another starship and are entertaining such plans themselves. The stars, beckon."

"What do we do with the Elders once we get them back here on Zannia?" Meta asked.

"Good question. I think they will be delighted to be here, although it may seem a bit awkward with the political changes."

"The passing of time will take care of that," Brock interjected. "After all, they were working diligently to get back to Zannia when the disaster happened."

Mentar nodded. "I think they will spend the rest of their days studying the planet to discover what caused its demise and then how it rebounded when we abandoned it many millennia ago. There's also talk of a group of researchers from Earth, *little ones*, that want to study Zannia and then return home. They will be here for one year."

Mingee joined in: "Some of the Elders may want to stay on Earth."

"Perhaps," Mentar agreed. "I'm sure the *little ones* will allow them to join our colonists that we are delivering. The *little ones* will benefit from the knowledge of the Elders. In fact, they probably already have. Also; the Elders that return here, which will be most of them, will be quite valuable as historians. It's important that our young know our full history. The happenings in the Solar System literally changed our civilization."

Little One was outfitted for a journey to Earth. Mentar was on the bridge, going over the final departure checklist. It had taken three months of hard work to get the crew and colonists ready and load provisions for their permanent stay on Earth.

A group of 300 colonists had been picked, along with those that were born on Earth and in route to Zannia and their families who wanted to lay eyes on the world of the *little ones* one more time.

Satisfied that all was in order, Mentar was about to give the departure order, but he was interrupted by a verbal message from the Peak Island station. The operator seemed overly excited.

"Mentar, this is Peak Island, over!"

Mentar keyed in. "Yes, this is Mentar?"

"Sir, we just received an urgent message from the President of the United States, on Earth. He instructed us to deliver it to you immediately."

"A personal message…it must be important. Yes, transmit it to my communications console here on the ship."

"Yes, sir…sending it now."

The message appeared on Mentar's screen. As he read it, he caught his breath. The bridge crew had never seen what Mentar did next. He lowered his head, lifted his massive hand to his face, and covered his eyes. There was a slight shuttering in his shoulders. The crew looked back and forth at each other, as they slowly gathered near the monitor. They were close enough to read the message:

"Dear Mentar. We have recovered the second ship from the waters below Easter Island. The crew of four are alive and well. There was a fifth passenger, not listed on their manifest, who is also alive and well. He is a teenager. We have confirmed his name. It is... Menvaar Ataar Kaavienne. Congratulations! The son awaits his reunion with his father."

The crew returned to their duty stations, allowing Mentar time to process the news. Most were unaware that Mentar had a son. He had never spoken of it. His close associates had noticed a slight cloud of sadness in his demeanor, but assumed it had to do with the loss they had all felt, when their rescuers had given them the news of the total destruction of their world.

Finally, Mentar lifted his head. The moisture in his eyes was overshadowed by the new smile on his face. He looked at Little One's Pilot. "On my command, engage all rotor pods! Three, two, one...ENGAGE!"

With all aboard, the starship set sail for Earth. Peak Island beamed the message toward Earth. It would arrive three years before Little One would deliver the father to the son.

Kronos, Mentar's Vice President, remained on Zannia and assumed the center seat of its governing body.

DAN HOLT & MAX HOLT

Chapter 11

Fourteen Years Old

Benjamin Franklin High School

New Orleans, Louisiana

The Principle looked up from his work as his secretary walked into the office. He *knew* the look on her face. He laid his pen down and sat back.

"Who is it this time?"

"Juan."

He rolled his eyes. "Valencia…again? He didn't break another restroom door, did he?"

"No sir…fighting. He's been bullying the Jenkins kid. Billy's friends were waiting this time and they all took on Juan. He took half of them down before they finally bloodied his nose. Then, they dragged him down here. Now, the janitor will have to clean the blood off my floor! Sir, I don't want to tell you your job, but isn't it time to just kick him out?"

"Believe me, that would be my choice, but it isn't that simple."

She shook her head. "It's the District again, isn't it? Why don't they just let us do our jobs?"

He smiled. "They are pretty much clueless…none of them have spent much time at the school level. They don't know what it's like to deal with these problems every day. They've put Juan under that new welfare

91

initiative the Justice Department created for this year. His dad is an ex-con...uh...pardon my lapse in propriety...his is a rehabilitated prisoner. Justice decided to fund the education of their children, in an attempt to foster their success. They think it will help them become better productive members of society." He collected his thoughts. "Okay, send him in."

A few moments later, Juan entered his office and plopped down in the most distant chair from his desk. He looked around the office, avoiding eye contact. His eyes were red and watery, obviously from the big swollen and bloody nose. His jeans were dirty and torn and his t-shirt was soaked in dried blood, covering most of the Hell's Angels logo on the front. His knuckles were bruised and bloody.

"Nice office," he said, almost nonchalantly. Of course, he had seen it several times before.

The Principle drug an empty chair over and sat directly in front of the boy. He waited for Juan to make eye contact.

"Juan, listen, this can't go on. First, the fire in the Science Lab garbage can, and then they caught you spiting in the soup in the cafeteria. The restroom door already cost the school $500. We know you've been bullying Billy Jenkins, and now there's blood all over you and half his friends. What am I going to do with you?"

Juan looked up. "Nobody likes me here; I don't like anybody here. Kick me out."

"Don't think I haven't thought of that, but that's not the answer. I really don't get it. I've looked out my window and seen you put a soccer ball in the goal from 50 yards out, but you've never put on a jersey. The PE Coach says you make 75 percent of your shots from the three-point circle, but you won't join the team. The Computer Lab teacher says you make an **A** on every programming test and you understand computer code better than most high-schoolers. But, you refuse to participate on one of her programming teams."

Juan cracked a sly smile. "I'm smarter than they are...I like to work alone."

"That may be true, but you can't go on thumbing your nose at society forever."

Juan bristled as he straightened up. "They thumbed their nose at my grandpa, he was an astronaut...and at my dad. He was just doing what he thought was right. I'm not going to let them get away with it. My time will come!"

The Principle had read the back-story about Juan when the new welfare program enrolled him in Ben Franklin. "Juan, starting tomorrow, I am going to pull you out of PE once a week for the next two months to talk with Mrs. Owenby, the school counselor. You will meet with her and work out some of this anger you seem to have. If you don't get your mind straightened out soon, you'll be in trouble for the rest of your life."

Juan cracked another smile on his bloody lips, "Yeah...whatever."

The Principle sat back, thinking about this troubled teen. Then, he remembered a recent news report. "So, your grandfather was an astronaut?"

Juan, on edge, looked him in the eye, ready to defend his grandfather's legacy. "Yeah, what of it?"

"How would you like to be an astronaut?"

Juan's eyes brightened. "What do you mean? How?"

"You know about the giants from Easter Island and that they are now in Mentar City. The government has announced plans to exchange colonies with the giants...us on Zannia and them in a permanent colony in Mentar City. They'll be working on that for several years."

"What's that got to do with being an astronaut? I don't want to get involved with those giants. They got my grandpa and dad all messed up."

"Juan, listen, some of the most important people the colony on Zannia will need are computer experts. Your teacher says you are the best computer coder and programmer she has seen in a high school freshman. Imagine, if you stopped getting in trouble all the time and buckled down on your computer studies, you might just qualify to apply for that colony. They said they'll be wanting to include minorities in the colony. Just think...with some work on your part, you could be out in space, on that ship headed for Zannia. You could be an astronaut...just like your grandfather."

"You really think so?!"

"I don't see why not. The choice is up to you, whether or not you will get yourself qualified. If I were in your shoes and could code like you can...I'd go for it."

Juan left the Principal's office with a new resolve, a new mission for his life. He still felt like an outsider but he decided that this new direction could eventually help him in his ultimate plan to *get even*.

So, he bided his time by obeying the Principle. He went for the weekly counseling with Mrs. Owenby, the social worker who did counseling for the school. He also drove his nose deeper into his computer studies.

When the school announced that the original space ship, Research One, had included New Orleans on their scheduled tour of the country, he was first in line to sign up for the on-board guided tour of the ship. His eyes widened as he walked up the ramp, into the machine that started it all. The glistening lights on the instrument panels and the humming of the rotor pod captured his imagination. He asked and was allowed to sit in the Computer Console seat. As he reached and touched the keyboard, he thought, *"Soon, Grandpa."* He then closed his eyes and saw…Zannia.

DAN HOLT & MAX HOLT

Chapter 12

Cosmos

Earth

Cosmos reached completion. Now, the technicians were going over the entire ship, especially the newly-added capabilities of supporting suspended animation. Many information-laced messages from Little One, as she flew the twenty-two-year journey to the Alpha Centauri System without the benefit of the extended sleep system, clearly supported its inclusion for extended space flight. There were many challenges that had to be dealt with that arose simply because a group of sentient beings were forcibly confined in a closed space for a long period of time.

Some ten years into the mission, many of the messages received from Little One contained the phrase: "It is better to sleep away the lightyears." So, Cosmos was outfitted with suspended animation units to accommodate up to two thousand souls; the set limit for the ship's complement for star travel. Also, a complete system for suspended animation was fabricated to outfit Little One upon her arrival on Earth. Not only would these systems greatly reduce the necessary consumables that have to be considered for any interstellar travel, but they also arrest the enemy of star travel—aging.

Chester Goldwin, NASA Administrator, stepped up to the podium to address NASA's planners on behalf of the president.

"Ladies and gentlemen, as you know, Mentar and Little One are due here in less than two years. Aboard are 300 colonists that will be remaining here on Earth. The Zannians are preparing accommodations, a town, for 300 Earthlings to return with them to Zannia. They call it Little One Village, Zannia. No surprise there.

"We are in process of selecting colonists to move to Zannia and remain there." Chester paused a moment and then continued. "One other chore that must be attended to, by the time Mentar and company arrive, is arranging for the Elders, the giants recovered from Easter Island, to take their ships with them to Zannia. They are going to leave four of the 160-footers and one of the cargo vessels. But, that still leaves 40 ships to get aboard Little One; eight cargo ships and thirty-two shuttles.

"Little One's largest access port to the cargo hold is 250 feet wide. The thirty-two smaller ships can be flown into the cargo hold and moored. The Elders offered to fly their cargo ships to Zannia using the suspended animation equipment. However, their ships cannot keep up with Little One and Cosmos. They are underpowered, relative to them, and would extend the journey for the crews back up to over twenty years. Therefore, the eight cargo ships will be dismantled and crated to fit in the cargo hold of Little One. Mr. Snyder, CEO of Snyder General Systems, has offered the needed warehouse space. He, if you remember, handled the salvaging of Zannia 2, a few years ago. Also, his son, Captain Snyder flies DOE 1 for the Air Force. We will have the Elders fly their ships to Aurora, Illinois, to Snyder's warehouses and dismantle them. There's a pad there where Little One can land and pick them up."

Colonel Jimmy Austin, selected to command Cosmos, stood on the bridge of the starship with his crew. There had been a detailed and extensive selection process to assemble what he and the planners at NASA felt would be a crew best suited for planet Earth's first venture to the stars. The primary bridge crew and a backup were recruited from Discovery, the Maxie Gene, and the Mary Lou along with a support staff of hundreds that were available when the salvaging operation of the Zannia 2 was completed. DOEs 1 and 2 were assigned to Cosmos along with their respective crews.

Cosmos incorporated thirty-six decks. Sixteen were a giant greenhouse for growing the food supply for the ship's company. Its by-product—oxygen. Twenty decks were for all other needs of a mobile world. Deck four was a sea of containers for suspended animation, 2000 of them, each with a timer.

The planners worked out a schedule for groups of people to share the necessary awake time. A practice to lessen the aging of the crew on the long journey to destination.

An outer ring; an outside containment tank, was added to the ship's hull to store the special agent for suspended animation. It was a giant donut that circled the entire ship, minus a gap for the massive windshield and three smaller gaps for the port holes, port, starboard, and aft. Additionally, it was separate from the ship's atmosphere, outside the hull, as a safety factor. The design resulted in four separate tanks.

Colonel Austin looked at his crew. They were all seasoned bridge personnel on this type of craft. They had flown thousands of hours during the Zannia 2 salvaging operation, had experienced weightlessness, pressure suits, *zero-G* and *near-zero-G* sleeping, eating, and *zero-G* personal hygiene. The one thing new here, the thing they were discussing among themselves at this moment, was dealing with four-times the mass when maneuvering Cosmos. "During the next month," the colonel instructed, "you will be schooled in the function of the sensor array and the Magnetic Field Generator on Cosmos. Six weeks from now we will fly her to the edge of space for a shakedown."

Chester Goldwin, NASA Administrator, contacted the original crew of Research One and petitioned them to come and fly the maiden voyage to the edge of space in Cosmos. He informed the Records Department and the Public Relations Officer to record and officiate the entire voyage for television, for those land-bound viewers that funded Cosmos, and for live streaming on the Internet. Two of the shuttles from Discovery would do the honors from outside the starship to record the initial flight. The effort would, no doubt, increase the viewership of the NASA Channel, or Giants' Channel, as it was called early on during the Saga.

Mentar City

As the weeks rolled by, the Elders at Mentar City watched the hundreds of trucks approach the starship, be unloaded onto motorized trolleys, and then drive away. Hundreds of the 10x10x50 wax cakes were ferried by the guppies to the holding tanks around the perimeter of the ship and loaded on board. Cosmos could now reach another star. The power plant of the ship made it possible. A principle of physics that the Elders had missed. Though they were learned and brilliant, one could not know everything. They had not realized, as the earthman, Frank Gordon, had, that adding the influence of magnets to their capture of inertial force would increase the power substantially. When they got home, they would have a new world to consider. A new world indeed.

They wondered what Zannia looks like now. Information gleaned from historical records, now buried under rubble on the moon, indicated that it was virtually barren when it was abandoned in a spaceship that took 75 years to build. Zannia had become a barren world dotted with pedestal cities and oxygen-separating plants lining the ocean shores. Seventy-five percent of the food was being wrenched from the dwindling offerings of the ocean. Thousands had fled to search for a new home. Fortunately, at the time, the closest star, Sol, and its family of planets was a haven of bounty.

Frank Gordon's exact duplicate of the original Research One arrived at the Space Flight Center and construction site of Cosmos. The original crew that had flown the first mission to the moon, following the end of the Apollo program many years earlier, were invited to be on the maiden flight of America's, and planet Earth's, first interstellar starship. They boarded the ship and were escorted to the bridge.

Colonel Jimmy Austin, commanding Cosmos, keyed the intercom. "Ship's company, we are honored to have the original crew that flew to the moon and made the discovery that launched America and the rest of the world into the era of reaching for the stars. Colonel Marvin Andrews, Douglas Hastings, Frank Gordon, David Henson, Daniel Stubblefield, and, in the custody of his son, David Henson, the remains of late Isaac Jacob Henson, Research One's Safety Officer. His son felt he would want to be included on this voyage."

Applause slowly spread, then filled the ship. Colonel Austin looked around at his crew and gave the order to prepare for launch. The Computer Control Systems Officer pushed the button marked **Power**. The computer began starting the 150 rotor pods as Katy Baylor watched the indicator lights flash red, then turn green, ten seconds apart. In just under half an hour Cosmos was at full power. Bruce Wilson, pilot, typed in **100 MILES** on the **Y Axis** of the control center and then waited for the launch order.

Colonel Austin turned to the man that started it all; Douglas Charles Hastings: "Mr. Hastings, would you honor us by giving the launch order?"

Doug glanced around at his fellows and then complied: "Launch Cosmos."

The starship rose majestically straight up from the earth and punched a half-mile-wide hole in the fluffy white clouds of central Kansas. The white mist bellowed in behind the ship in a salute. Jimmy noticed that the two shuttles assigned to record the event, having patched into Cosmos' flight computer, rose simultaneously with the starship. Far below was the postage-stamp-sized launching pad and just to the side, a very tiny Mentar City.

Cosmos came to a stop and hovered at 100 miles. The two accompanying shuttles backed away for a distance to record the overall activity of the shakedown for the documentary-style account. The various crews spent the next several hours testing all systems in their areas of responsibility.

All excursion craft, the six shuttles and six guppies were pressurized, launched to circle the mother ship, and then return to their respective hangar bays, a trek of just under two miles. Aboard Shuttle One was a team from Ship's Records to capture digital records for its files, as well as for prime-time television. The two DOEs, though proven many time over, joined in with a launch and circumnavigation of Cosmos to prove their hangar doors and atmospheric pressure systems, and then returned to their special hangar bay.

Jimmy, monitoring the activity, noted again the small golf-cart-type electric vehicle parked at the end of the bridge. It was of a very light tubular construction, designed to carry four people. It was first designated as a run-about; then finally the name that stuck was R-bot. It had large hollow magnetic wheels to keep it safely in place during weightless periods. He glanced at it momentarily, then looked across the vast main deck of the ship. "A prudent addition," he thought. From the bridge to the aft lounge was half-a-mile. A long walk. He noted that there was one parked at most of the clusters of work stations.

Another plus for the special vehicle; one could grab one of the notorious Goop Guns, a special tool developed for sealing any minor hull breach, board the vehicle, strap in, and drive up the wall, across the ceiling, and tend to any damage that might otherwise be out of reach without a series of ladders. When the unit was first completed and brought on board for testing, the engineers drove around on the ceiling and played catch with a basketball. It was quite a trick to toss the ball in an inverted arc. They had to have a volunteer to *work the floor*—tossing a missed ball back to many waiting hands extended down from the ceiling.

Daniel Stubblefield viewed the horizon and curvature of the earth for a long moment, then glanced at Marvin, Doug, and Dave. "I remember the first time I saw this. It was a defining moment for me. It's still just as mesmerizing."

"Yeah, yeah it is," Marvin said. "This crew and the colonists, with this ship, are going to see a new horizon. What a moment that will be. If you watch this crew, they are almost walking above the floor. Oh, to be young again."

Frank joined in. "Gentlemen," he said, "we were lucky enough to live in a special time. I am content to watch these young explorers carry on. I say God Speed."

"Hear—hear!" came from all.

DAN HOLT & MAX HOLT

Chapter 13

The School

Mentar City

Connie Maeson was burning the midnight oil, pouring over the final 500 applicants for the Earth Colony on Zannia, scheduled to depart; exact date, uncertain. Over 10,000 Earthlings had applied to journey to the stars with Earth's first colony. Only 300 would be chosen. She had a lot of work to do; the first 50 selected had to be announced by next week.

As a retired school teacher and District Superintendent, Connie considered herself to be a fair, but no-nonsense person. Years earlier, she had been the third-grade teacher of the President's youngest son. He was impressed with her professionalism, so he called her out of retirement and asked her to run the show. The selection process had been grueling, and far too political for her tastes.

People from 90 percent of the world's countries and all of the USA states had applied. Politics came in when some countries *called in favors*, convincing the President to get involved in the selection process. Of course, gender came into play, family units had to be carefully screened and ethnicities had to be represented.

Juan Valencia was now 18. He had planned for this day since age nine. Finally, he was sure he would be in a position to *get even* for the wrong that had been done to his family. For the last nine years, he had learned to take care of himself. He didn't bother with making *real* friends, he just concentrated on *today*. He had researched and analyzed what the most demanded skills would be for the colony he planned to be part of. He deduced that two of the critical elements of an extended space flight and a permanent colony were communications and computer skills. So, he poured himself into those subjects in school.

At age 17, he applied for the colony, registering for ethnic minority status, knowing that would give him a slight edge over many others. When the first two groups of 50 names were announced, and he was not on either list, he decided to apply one of the *skills* he had learned from his dad…breaking and entering. He broke into the Colony Planning Office and found his file in one of the piles of applicants. He removed a couple of new *faked* documents from his pocket, slipped them in the middle of the file and then sneaked it into Mrs. Maeson's office, placing it within 10 of the top. He called his ailing dad and got the congratulations he expected.

When the next list was released, he was number 37 of the 50. He mentally made a *checkmark* and started planning his next step. He knew it would have to include one of the giants he had met; one of the survivors from the depths off Easter Island. He remembered his name...Yaccavan. It was time to make friends.

Juan met Yaccavan during the interviews associated with the Colony Application process. The planners had decided that the two-year Colonist Preparation School would need to include giants of various ages, to help the earth colonists get adjusted to living with the giant population on Zannia. So, they paired potential colonists with some of the giants, to interview together and spend some recreation time together, to see if there were any *hidden* prejudices that might come out later. Juan knew what they were up to, so he made sure to *play nice* and be seen as nonbiased.

In reality, he didn't care much for the giants. None of them had ever been rude or harmed him in any way but he blamed their presence on the moon for being the reason his grandfather had made the drastic decision as an astronaut, leading to his act being brought to the public and, ultimately, to him taking his own life.

Yaccavan's age was uncertain, but he was a teenager, by giant standards, being just 30 feet tall. When the giants' ships had descended to their Easter Island *graves*, some 50,000 years ago, he had been a communications and computer systems trainee on Kavientar's ship. He had resisted the assignment but his father had insisted. In the giants' culture, fathers were always obeyed. Yaccavan's resistance had to do with his perception of how his father had been disrespected by the Elders.

His father had been recommended for selection as an Elder in the giants' government. He had all of the necessary qualifications; the Upper-Level School and the recommendation of his personal mentor. But, as also happened on Earth, another, more popular candidate was chosen over him. The giant had seemed unfazed by the rejection, but his son, Yaccavan, became angry; out of character for the giants' culture. He wanted to get back at his superiors for the disrespecting of his father, but he had no idea how…until he met Juan.

Yaccavan appreciated how the *little ones* had rescued them from eventual death but he had no particular affinity for the tiny Earthlings. They seemed to always be in the way and all giants had been cautioned to watch where they were walking, so as not to accidently crush one of their fragile bodies. He didn't like being in the Colony School with them, although he understood the need for orienting them on what to expect on Zannia. He too, didn't know what to expect, having never been there either.

But, the day Yaccavan met Juan, he liked him. They both had had communications and computer training and had scored high in all related areas. Yaccavan also saw in Juan a slight *rebellion* that he felt himself. He knew they would get along. Juan soon felt the same way. He had finally met someone who would be able to understand how he felt. As they got to know each other and shared their *less than normal* backgrounds, they started making plans on how to make the trip to Zannia...*uncomfortable* for the leaders...to somehow *make them pay* for the wrongs done to their fathers.

DAN HOLT & MAX HOLT

Chapter 14

Preparations

Twenty-five light-hours from Earth

Mentar sat, staring at the pale blue dot on Little One's long range viewer. Earth. He had friends there. He would see them soon. Ship's remaining travel time—decelerating—just over ten months. The transit time Zannia to Earth was still very long, although the improved speed did make a lot of difference. He would be glad to have the animation equipment in the ship to sleep away the miles.

A notice of an incoming message sounded on the communications console. Mentar touched the control. It was a message from Earth, from Colonel Andrews. *"Is Javienne, the musician, on board?"*

Mentar brought up a response screen: *"Yes, he is. He has a six-member band now—four of them singers. They have learned Earth's and Zannia's favorite song and will play and sing it as a group. I think Earth calls it a quartet."* Mentar clicked **Send**. The message would arrive in one day; Little One, in ten months.

Waiting for Mentar on Earth was a real test of his leadership and governing ability of a society; a civilization. In his past interactions with the Elders, brief but engaging, they were always treated as absolute, especially those that were members of the Solaris 4 government. In the Solaris 4 political system, there were the People, the Elders, and the Government.

Further, the government was always chosen from the Elders. The Elders: all over 50 and highly educated. New members of the Elders were determined by the current Elders. It was so engrained that it was even supported by all the populace. *It's the way things were.*

But now, the lifeways, behavior, motives, and actions of the *little ones* of Earth had lifted the curtain off Mentar's mind and eyes. He remembered what their late Professor Charles Liggins had said to him one time in passing. The professor was quoting one of the *little one's* historical figures: *"Nothing is either good or bad, but thinking makes it so."* He now had to be able to explain himself to the Elders. They deserved a chance to understand why Zannia's political system was changed.

Mentar had assumed the office of President, as requested by the people, for early stability. Then, his parliament was selected, again, by the people. The system would grow from there. Would the Elders be angry, upset, rebellious, or perhaps, relieved?

Ship-to-Earth messaging had ascertained that Mentar would get to see, once again, Colonel Andrews and his crew. Seeing them again would be good, very good. There was something special about interstellar friends.

The Frank Gordon Space Flight Center
Wichita, Kansas, 10 months later

Earth began preparing to greet friends from afar. A party in the shadow of a starship.

Cosmos was moved from its construction pad over to the vast tarmac of the Space Flight Center. The construction pad was cleared for Little One, for the alteration of adding the suspended animation equipment. Mentar was collecting a barter arrangement for the updated sensor array and Magnetic Field Generator he had freely shared with Earth.

Little One would be landing in three days, at about noon. The surrounding area was being prepped for onlookers that would be there by the thousands. The return of the giants had been on all the airways for the past month. The reunion of all time. The *little ones* would get to see them again and they, the giants, would be reunited with their Elders.

There were rumors galore of father and son, mother and daughter, and all combinations that would see each other again after they had assumed that they were all dead. Of the 180 surviving Elders, there were 17 confirmed cases of offspring, alive and well and all aboard Little One.

The first two came to light with the helter-skelter flight to the moon by Kaatar and Letar, upon being awakened from their watery grave. They had been escorted there and back as a precaution during the early hours of the first contact with the Elders. That incident triggered a prudent inquiry by Dwight Cummins, the president's liaison, resulting in the list of kin on their way from Zannia.

Dwight had shown Kaatar the birth notice that had been radioed to Discovery, years earlier, while it was in route to Saturn; the birth announcement of his grandson. Kaatar read it: "*Live birth. Male. Aledo Mentar Kaavienne. Five-feet-four-inches long. Eighty-two pounds, six and one-half ounces. Born planet Earth.*"

Dwight had looked up at him and had spoken in Moon: "You're a grandfather. Congratulations. Your grandson, Aledo Mentar, is now thirty-five years old. He and your daughter are aboard Little One."

Kaatar had sat down to deal with his emotions. Dwight made a strategic exit.

Chapter 15

Arrival

Frank Gordon Space Flight Center
Control Tower

The Duty Sergeant's eyes snapped to the radar screen when the alarm sounded. A new blimp had appeared. Beside it was a flashing designation: *Unknown.* He grabbed a pair of binoculars and searched the sky. "I see it! It's coming out of the Southwest!"

His colleague also grabbed a pair and located the approaching ship. "Call the Administrator and let him know. Little One is approaching."

The announcement went out to the masses. Thousands of eyes went to the Southwest, searching for the advancing spaceship from another star. Soon, sporadically, young eyes began spotting the pin dot and pointing. The half-mile diameter starship soon began to dominate the sky. Thousands held up their arms and hands toward the sky in a victory cheer.

Little One approached and hovered over the launching pad. Adjacent to it was a raised platform supporting the President, his liaison, the NASA Administrator, Colonel Andrews and his crew, and five representatives of the 180 Elders of Mentar City. Standing with the Elders, trying not to show what he was feeling, was Menvaar, now eight years older, but still his father's son, needing the embrace of those massive arms.

The remainder of the giants, now into the eighth year of their tenure in Mentar City, were gathered on the north side of the special-sized metropolis, next to the launching pad. All those that had family members arriving on Little One were informed. Their counterparts aboard the arriving starship had also been informed on who was waiting to see them. Aledo Mentar Kaavienne, 35, slowly made his way toward the front of the group. He wanted to be one of the first to disembark when signaled. He wanted to see if he would recognize his grandfather. He was 100.

The onlookers watched the twenty-seven landing struts appear from the under belly of the craft and lower and lock themselves. Dwight Cummins was giving a move-by-move account over the PA system, for the sake of the onlookers unable to get a clear visual. Little One settled gently on the pad. There were several moments of pressure equalization to Earth's atmosphere. Giants inside Little One began gathering at the portholes and waving at the crowd. Cheers went up as they were spotted by the onlookers.

Moments later the massive ramp was lowered and the upper door rose to full open. Mentar led the way as he, Brock, Mingee, and Meta came walking down the ramp. Hearing the roar of the crowd, they stopped and waved to the masses. Mentar then continued down the ramp and approached the raised platform. He saw the mature young giant, no longer a child. A hush fell on the crowd. Anticipating the reunion of the century, the media was enjoying the best ratings in a decade…2.7 billion Earthlings had tuned in.

Mentar approached Menvaar. The son, showing his maturity, extended his right hand, palm out, toward the left shoulder of his father, to give the traditional greeting of their culture. Mentar smiled, disregarded the greeting, and practiced what the *little ones* had taught him 40 years earlier; he hugged his son. The crowd's applause was thunderous for 10 minutes. Landfills all over the earth would soon receive 2.7 billion tear-stained tissues.

Finally, Colonel Andrews stepped forward, cradled his hands on his hips, stepped to the edge of the platform, and looked up at Mentar. "Hello, big guy."

"Hello, Little One."

The roar of applause began again and lasted minutes. Mentar nodded to the President: "Mr. President, it's good to be here again. I hope you have been well."

"Thank you, Mentar. How was your trip?"

"Still long, especially when Menvaar was waiting." He still had his arm around him. "Little One is a good ship, however, we need to make a change."

"I heard. Sleeping equipment is ready for installation."

Mentar paused for a moment, then stepped over to the five representative giants from the Elders at Mentar City. He established eye-to-eye contact with the older of the representatives, then, in a deliberate gesture, extended his hand, officially introducing Earth-

119

greetings into their culture. The Elderly giant, looked down at his hand momentarily, then took it. Mentar spoke in Moon; then looked from face to face of the Elders, then spoke again in English: "Welcome back from the brink of extinction. And, thank you for saving my son."

The Elder spoke: "Mentar, we are at somewhat of a loss. I am Maaelienvar, I was experimenting with robot control for Zannia 2 for the journey home when Solaris 4 exploded and..."

"I imagine that was quite a shock," Mentar interrupted. "We'll discuss our situation at length in the next few days. Right now, I must tend to some business."

Mentar signaled his officer standing on the ramp of Little One. He nodded. Shortly, the ship's occupants came streaming down the ramp, looking around at the open sky and at the crowd of *little ones* attending the arrival. Next, they spotted their fellow giants standing between the pad and Mentar City and headed in that direction.

When Kaagan saw the giants disembarking Little One, he made his way to the front of the group of waiting Elders. Momentarily, he spotted Aledo. It was like looking in a mirror, a kind mirror. Aledo was in the likeness of his grandfather, minus the effects of aging and the marks of 100 years of relentless gravity. Kaagan raised his hand and arm and called his name. Aledo saw his grandfather and quickened his step.

Over the next hour, that scene was repeated sixteen more times.

President Mitchell, watching the giants exit Little One and stream toward Mentar City, leaned toward Dwight, his liaison. "A historic moment for planet Earth."

Dwight Cummins nodded then spoke in Moon. The president looked at him. He repeated himself in English: "Yes, sir."

The president paused a moment. "It's strange that you would do that; especially at this moment."

"It was spontaneous, sir. I didn't mean to be coy."

"Dwight, I wonder if one day there might be a Galactic language, that all must learn."

"I would say that that would be far in the future. Many years ago, about the middle of last century, there was a dubious flirtation with the scientists creating a universal language for Earth and having everyone learn it. It didn't last long. They encountered two big problems. One: all peoples love the language of their birth. And two: the voice box of the speaker of every language is shaped for that particular language. The result; when one speaks a different language, word sounds are different. Accent is created. Some of the accents are so pronounced that a native of that language cannot understand a foreign speaker of it."

"All the people on Zannia speak the same language."

"Yeah," Dwight agreed. "Yet they created the different languages that are spoken on Earth."

121

"Intentional or not, they made Earth unique. What else is out there in the cosmos?"

"Everything," Dwight responded quietly.

Chapter 16

The Conference

Earth's preparation for Little One over the past months came to fruition on arrival day. The ship touched down a few minutes after noon. By 2:00 p.m., the salutations were finished and the ship's company and the colonists had disembarked and were interacting in Mentar City. The President, NASA, the Commander of Cosmos and his bridge crew, Colonel Andrews, and his crew of the original Research One, were in the conference room *catching-up* with and getting to know Mentar and his company.

Outside, a couple hundred volunteers were setting up a stage, sound equipment, seats, podiums, and monitors for an evening of festivities; an interstellar party under and around a visiting starship. There were several speakers scheduled, then Javienne's band and, as suggested by Colonel Andrews, a band picked by call-in voting—The Mooners.

When the Mooners learned that they had won the spot in the celebration, they wrote and learned to sing in Moon and English: **No Distance is too Far.**

The celebration began at 6:00 p.m. and lasted until after midnight. Then, a shipload of weary travelers went to their respective accommodations to sleep, for

123

the first time in years, on the surface of a planet, under a star.

Mentar City Conference Room

Mentar sat at the conference table. To his right was Brock, the historian and leader of Zannia's Department of Education. On his left were Mingee and Meta, Agriculture and Population Planning in Zannia's government. Across the table were Maaelienvar and several of his engineering team. Dwight Cummins was in his place to listen and advise the President. Mentar called the meeting to order. The conference room got quiet. Mentar addressed the Elders.

"Maaelienvar, how many of your 180 that survived the Easter Island sleep, are government officials?"

"None," Maaelienvar responded. "All the selected members of government had left about six months before the explosion. They went from Mars to the Moon, remained there a month, then they returned to Solaris 4. Apparently, they all perished there with the rest of the governing forum. Why, Mentar?"

"Zannia's government has been reorganized to be operated by the will of the people; *all* the people. Everyone is expected to honor its laws and regulations."

"Of course," Maaelienvar said then added: "We are scientists. Our concern is the pursuit of science. We leave the political pursuits to the government. By the way, you solved the conveyance problem back to

Zannia quite nicely. While waiting for you, we learned about the deal you made with the *little ones,* for that ship. We've never heard of such a concept."

"I learned it from the *little ones.* Their society operates on a medium of exchange. They call it money. I offered them the bounty on Zannia 2, the precious metals in her drive, which have monetary value here on Earth. They accepted and built a ship of sufficient size and capability to reach Zannia. The *little ones* had a breakthrough in propulsion technology. Also, they had a great need for the precious metals. You will find them quite an interesting and marvelous people."

"We already have. I have lectured all across their land."

"You, all of you, have much of the same to do back home on Zannia. The people of Zannia are very lucky that you were found and revived. Upon arrival at Zannia, we need for you to commit to books and files all your knowledge of our history, science, accomplishments, and social development for instruction of our young."

"We look forward to it."

DAN HOLT & MAX HOLT

Chapter 17

The Module

Kavientar, following the conference, asked to meet privately with Mentar. They met in Mentar's quarters on Little One.

"Mentar, he said, "Over these years, as guests of the *little ones*, we have learned to respect them and their development into intelligent, creative beings. You and the students were most fortunate to be discovered and rescued. Had the small group of *little ones* not been bold enough to determine the truth about their moon, all of you…and all of us, would surely have perished at some future date, when the sleeping gas was depleted."

Mentar nodded. "Yes, fate smiled on us when Douglas Hastings studied closely NASA's photos of the moon. As you say, these *little ones* do indeed deserve respect for what they have accomplished." He hesitated. "But, I don't think you asked to meet with me just to praise their progress. I sense that there is another reason for this meeting."

Kavientar looked toward the door, as if to verify it was closed. "Yes, Mentar, I want to..uh, I *need* to know if you were able to acquire the Module from the vault in the lab on the moon. As you know, my ancient relatives were given charge of it, even before they abandoned Zannia for the planets of Sol. I witnessed the transfer of it to my father and received that responsibility myself, just before my father died on Solaris 4, long before the disaster."

Mentar just stared, not sure what to say.

Kavientar saw the confusion on his face. "Mentar, you do know what I'm referring to, don't you?"

Mentar shook his head. "No, I don't."

Kavientar sat back and hesitated, then spoke. "I was told that the senior leaders of all areas of our society were informed about the Module and its history. That would have included the counselors as well."

"Perhaps the senior counselors on the moon were aware of this *Module*, but I was a new counselor and had just brought a group of student trainees to the moon before Solaris 4 was destroyed. Perhaps the elder counselors had not had time to inform me about it."

Kavientar hesitated, and then began. "This will take some time but it is very important that you understand. Eons before our ancestors began treating our home in an irresponsible way, depleting the sustainable bounty that we needed, our society built many beautiful structures that provided shelter and facilities for government and business. They had dug many mining tunnels under the nearby mountains to harvest the Zolaadine required for the pedestals to support our buildings.

"In one of the newer tunnels, our digging machine broke into a small cavern. To their surprise, the space was lit brightly, although they could not determine the source of the light. On a rock ledge there was a medal box. When they opened it, there was a long cylinder, made from some type of glass. It was 20 feet long and two feet in diameter. You can see crystalline spheres embedded inside it. It appeared to be built in three sections, tapered on each end and with an opening at one end, as though it was intended to be connected to something else.

"Inside the lid of the box were instructions in an unknown language. Researchers were unable to decipher it and determine what the object was or what it was meant to do.

Mentar leaned forward. "What did they do?"

"The Elders continued their research for many years but could not determine the true meaning of the message. They decided that at some time in the future, its meaning and the intended use of the Module would become clear.

Obviously, someone put it there; perhaps, one day, they would return. So, they decided to enlist a family-unit to take charge of it, to protect it by passing it from father to son, until its intended purpose could be realized. My great-great-grandfather's grandfather was chosen as the first in the line of Protectors. I was the last, before our existence was almost extinguished. So, you see, I have the responsibility to recover it and continue passing it down my family line until...*that day.*"

Mentar was reaching for his communications device, allowing connection to the earth's telephone system. "I will contact Douglas Hastings now and ask if such a container was found during their harvest of moon artifacts. In their state, called Colorado, they have a large storage facility carved underneath a mountain where they stored many of the moon artifacts and the bounty from Zannia 2. Perhaps he will be aware of this Module."

Mentar called Doug. Doug confirmed that neither he, nor any member of crews collecting artifacts from the moon, had ever seen such an item. He asked to meet with Mentar and Kavientar to better understand what they were looking for. Within 30 minutes, he was entering Little One.

Doug spoke to Kavientar. "Tell me, where would this special artifact have been stored on the moon? Mentar mentioned the Lab when he called. I walked into all of the accessible spaces and never saw what he described."

Kavientar took out a schematic from the records box that Kaagan and Letar had retrieved from the moon, when they were first brought up from the depths at Easter Island. He spread it on Mentar's table. "This is a depiction of the under-surface facilities in the Arcology on the moon." He pointed to a large wide tunnel. It was one of the first tunnels Doug and crew had entered, that had the giants in suspended animation.

Doug leaned in. "Yes, I remember that tunnel. It is still intact, we found most if the alive-students there."

Kavientar pointed to an area on the wall, a third if the way down the tunnel. "Did you see a doorway on the wall in this area?"

"Not that I recall. We were so focused on rescue that we may not have seen it."

Kavientar paused. "I need you to accompany me and Mentar on one more trip to your moon. I must retrieve the Module."

One hundred and forty miles above the Moon

Mentar's personal shuttle came to a hover, allowing Kavientar to take in the scene. He was quiet and reflective as he saw the vast destruction. Doug and Mentar allowed him time to process the feeling of loss that all who survived had to go through. Finally, Kavientar nodded and Mentar continued the approach.

For the first stop, Kavientar had requested to visit the Memorial Monument and pay his respects to the those who were entombed there. After a time of reflection and showing of respect, they continued to the objective.

Once inside, Mentar hovered slowly down the tunnel until Kavientar called for a halt. Although the glass suspended animation glass crates had been removed by Earth-crews, the support equipment remained. Behind two large pipes, on the wall, was a flat sealed door, that blended into the wall. Kavientar and Doug, already in pressure suits, went straight to the large door. Kavientar brushed the dust from a recessed handle, pulled it out and rotated it downward. The huge door slowly swung open.

As they entered the dark room, Doug turned on his light. There, in the center of a stone table, was the container Kavientar had described. He dusted the top and front of the box and undid the latches. He opened the box...the Module was still safely in place. He smiled and closed the lid. He gently rubbed his hands across it, as if caressing it, and then lifted the box and returned to the shuttle.

As the shuttle retraced its path, in preparation to depart the moon, Kavientar's eyes were glued to the windshield, still trying to reconcile the damage that had been done 50,000 years earlier. With his gaze still on the destruction, he said, "Mentar, I remember how refreshing it was back then, to return from an excursion to one of our test sites, and see the welcome site of the main entrance and the airlock back into the Archology. It was always a beautiful sight, like a breath of fresh air, as these *little ones* are prone to say."

Mentar nodded, "Yes, I remember, although I rarely had occasion to venture outside. But, that main entrance was beautiful."

Still looking at the landscape, Kavientar said, "If you would indulge me one last look at that area, I would be grateful."

"Yes, of course, although I am sure that it was also destroyed by the debris from Solaris 4."

Mentar changed course and flew slowly down the main road, leading to the main airlock. Just as he had said, the grand glass entrance and airlock lay in ruins, covered in the piles of lunar dirt that had been wrenched from the surface as the huge pieces of glass had impacted from above. Mentar flew out through the main area, and then reversed course to reenter the Archology from what would have been the outside. Suddenly, Kavientar called for a halt. Staring at the destroyed main entrance, he said, "Where is the sentinel?"

Hovering in place, Mentar scanned the area. "What sentinel?"

"The statue, brought here from Zannia 2, before we abandoned it in Saturn orbit. Remember, it was a symbol left on Zannia by the ancients, and then taken by the leaders when Zannia was determined uninhabitable. It was installed here, as a reminder of our heritage. Surely, no one had time to move it during the disaster."

Mentar set the shuttle down onto the surface. "We have time to search. Take Doug with you and see what you can find."

Kavientar and Doug suited up and processed outside. Following Kavientar's memory, they went to the largest pile of lunar soil, climbed up to the top and began pushing soil off and down the side. Finally, Doug helped him lift a large triangular piece of broken glass and push it over the side of the pile. As it slid down, it dragged a lot of soil with it. Kavientar turned to Mentar looking out through the windshield and gave a thumbs-up. As he stepped aside, they were all looking at the exposed head of a Moai.

Doug looked up. "How did this get here from Easter Island?!"

Kavientar shook his head. "It didn't. This is the one that we referenced when we carved the sentinels on the island; a message to the ones we were sure would rescue us. This sentential goes back at least 100,000 years in our history. Our historical records do not reveal where it came from or how long it has existed.

Mentar keyed his radio. "Kavientar, my friend, much of our history and our knowledge of the ancients has been lost. Rather than dwell on what we have lost, let us focus on what we have and what lies ahead."

With one last look at the stoic symbol of a past, never to be recovered, Kavientar returned to the ship.

Mentar set sail for Earth.

Mentar City, Conference Room

Mentar had radioed ahead, requesting a conference with both ships' crews and the leadership of both colonies. All met together in the Mentar City conference room. Kavientar displayed the historical Module and told all he knew about its history. The purpose of the meeting was to make sure that everyone knew of its existence and that it would accompany Kavientar to Zannia. He hoped that research and exploration on their home planet would someday reveal the true nature of this mysterious object.   After the meeting, the box was closed and locked and stored safely on Little One.

DAN HOLT & MAX HOLT

Chapter 18

The Crew

The Spacefarer's Club
Wichita, Kansas

Bruce Wilson, astronaut, Pilot. When Bruce joined NASA, his story soon got around. Bruce was born in Brad, Texas, population 40. When he turned sixteen years old, his parents moved to Red Oak, Texas, a suburb of Dallas, to find work. Bruce, found a job at a small suburban airport working after school and weekends fueling and cleaning small aircraft. The airport was dedicated to a club preserving the fixed wing, single engine, mode of flying during the advent of inertial propulsion. At seventeen he was given a special price on pilot training by a local flight instructor and soloed in eight hours.

Then, every week, he was able to commit five dollars for plane rental, a dollar a minute, at that time. He and his younger brother would push an ancient J3 cub two-passenger to the end of runway, get in, and start the aircraft, which would start the timer. They would enter the runway and take off and circle the field twice, then land, shut off the engine, and coast to a stop. Shutting off the engine stopped the timer at just under five dollars. Then, they would push the plane back to its tie-down spot. Bruce loved to fly. Now, he was going to fly all the way to another star.

Timothy Dalton, Copilot. Tim was recruited from the Navy. He performed well under pressure. The most notable entry on his service record was about him safely bringing in a plane onto an aircraft carrier, with a third of the right wing missing; a structural failure. He simply keeps thinking.

Katherine Baylor, Computer Control Specialist. Katy, at 18, was in her second year of college. At 22, she had a doctorate in computer science. She joined NASA immediately upon graduation.

Sharon Millar, Flight Safety Systems. Sharon mastered computer science. She also created an instructional pamphlet after spending many hours testing with mannequins on emergency positions during a strong avoidance maneuver. She discovered the best way to handle the event if you were caught out in the open when the ship made a powerful evasive maneuver: *Upon hearing the warning, drop to the floor and assume a fetal position on your side with your arms shielding you head.*

Melvin Faulkner, Telemetry. Melvin, a computer expert also, was a graduate of the Daniel Stubblefield Telemetry School.

Professionals all. It seemed that the advent of space flight had raised the ceiling on human capabilities. All coding classes were always at capacity. Colonel Jimmy Austin envisioned that in two or three more decades, the skies of Earth would be filled with saucers zipping here and there and with cars, as cross country conveyances, slowly dwindling away. He was thinking, *"It would be...*

"Colonel," Katherine Baylor said, "do we know the launch date to Zannia?"

"About a year. The suspended animation equipment must be finished on Little One and they are servicing all the rotor pods. Sounds like you are ready to go."

"Yes, sir. I want to watch the sun turn to a star; and then, watch the two stars of Alpha Centauri turn from stars to suns. And, I want to see Zannia. The giants describe it as a planet of lush growth, like the rain forest here, with pedestal cities in the sky. It must be beautiful."

DAN HOLT & MAX HOLT

Chapter 19

Launch

The Frank Gordon Space Flight Center

The two starships, Cosmos and Little One, sat a thousand feet apart on the tarmac of the Space Flight Center. They were loaded, prepped, and staffed for an eight-year journey to the Alpha Centauri star system. The guidance systems were linked electronically so that the two vessels would fly as one. As the miles rolled by, there would be excursion flights, one to the other, for various reasons while hurling through space at an ever-increasing velocity relative to their points of origin and destination. Twelve extra excursion craft were moored in Cosmos' cargo hold for use by the research scientists sent to study Zannia, then to be left behind when they returned to Earth. The colonists would need transportation.

Of the 180 Elders, 166 boarded Little One for the journey home to Zannia. The fourteen opting to remain on Earth were divided into two groups. Four of them were over 110 years old and just wanted to settle down for the duration and spend their last days counseling the young. They were hardily welcomed to remain in Mentar City with the colonists. The ten others, a self-appointed study group, wanted to investigate the population of Earth, the *little ones*, and learn how they developed their societies through the years, since their advent in the lab on the moon. Some of the nations were cautious about what it might involve. Others welcomed the spotlight. Most were indifferent but gave it the nod; perhaps it would result in additional curriculum for the schools.

The arriving colonists from Zannia spent a ceremonial time saying their final goodbyes to their friends aboard Little One; friends that they would likely not see again in their lifetimes. This parting was a repeat of a like-happening eight years earlier on Zannia and was happening now in the Cosmos camp. The colonists boarding Cosmos, although glad and eager to be a part of such a historical event, were deeply moved by the finality of their goodbyes.

One exception was Juan Valencia. He had hoped that his dad, Alan Brewster Jr., would somehow recover from his recent stay in the hospital and show up to give him a surprise goodbye. Instead, Juan discovered, when he called the hospital, that his dad had died during the night. The attending nurse got on the phone and told him that his dad had asked her to tell how proud he and his grandfather were of Juan's success. She was a little confused about Jr.'s final instruction to his son. She relayed that the old man had said, *"Do what you promised."*

Juan held back the tears that would flow from any *normal* son whose father had just died. But Juan was anything but normal. He just gritted his teeth and recommitted himself to his *quest*. Juan requested that the Hospital Administrator arrange his dad's funeral.

The government had granted sums of money to all colonists to help clear up their affairs before leaving Earth forever. The funds were allotted on a graduated scale...more for older couples with families and that had financial commitments to settle...less for young single colonists with no stated commitments. Juan's share was $500,000. He wired it all to the hospital, asking that the left-over amount be given to Benjamin Franklin High School in New Orleans, to be used to update their computer systems. Juan Valencia now had no reason to ever return to Earth.

The scientists were also boarding Cosmos to journey to Zannia, to study the planet for one year. Planet Earth wanted as much information about planet depletion and restoration as could be learned by the example of Zannia, which had successfully recovered from near dissolution. Therefore, any colonist that changed his or her mind would have a ticket home after one year on Zannia. Cosmos would be returning the researchers to Earth. It would be interesting to see the mindset of the colonists after one year away from Earth.

During the preparation phase, the President had enlisted a team of psychologists and population specialists to set the standards for the operation of the colony. This body had already screened all applicants who had professional skills and training, in order to select the leadership for the colony. After close screening and interviews, the team had selected a couple from New Orleans, Jack and Brenda Owenby, as Co-Presidents of the Earth Colony, Zannia. Jack had a background in city planning and administration and Brenda was a licensed psychologist, with a background as a Social Worker and School Counselor. They both had a zeal for adventure that made them the perfect choice for the leadership role.

The 300 colonists had been housed near the Space Flight Center in an apartment complex for three months before the scheduled departure date. They chose an advisory board of six, by popular vote. The Board would assist Jack and Brenda in the dad-to-day operations within the colony, both in route to and on Zannia.

Most of the colonists were family units with children varying in ages. Ten percent were chosen as single individuals, male and female, with little or no commitment to anyone, in an attempt to approximate a typical Earth subdivision of 300 residents.

When the chosen group met together earlier for their final detailed preparation, Benda sought out Juan. Juan, remembering his encounter with her when he was 14, was reluctant to engage with her. He was afraid she was going to share his background with the authorities and recommend he be deleted from the approved list.

Instead, she congratulated him on being selected. She said she was proud that he had followed the Principal's advice and refocused his life. She was looking forward to working with him as a fellow colonist.

She was impressed with his interest to study the computer systems on Cosmos.

If only she had known…

With the United States Marine Drum and Bugle Corps playing, and the President leading in a *goodbye wave,* Cosmos and Little One rose into the sky to begin an eight-year journey to Zannia. Little One had been this way before. However, this time, she was equipped with a new system; now, members of the crew could sleep away the day-to-day waiting for the vessel to traverse the endless miles to the next star.

During the first few days, the ship's company watched Mars go by, then the asteroid belt, only getting a glimpse of a couple of sizable members as they passed into the rear-view monitor. Then, they crossed the orbital planes of Jupiter, Saturn, and the other two gas giants, far in the distance. Their trajectory to Alpha Centauri was not exactly in line with the galactic plane. When they passed the orbit of the dwarf planet, Pluto, they would be as far from that world as they were the sun.

Mentar walked to the center of the main deck and looked upward. He saw what he knew it would be; an immense star field. Little One would find home; she knows where it is. He keyed the ship-to-ship for an operational status with Cosmos, and then headed for the newly renovated deck; the suspended animation equipped floor. He would close his eyes, and then wake up one year from now; a pact he had agreed upon with Colonel Austin. It would seem to be a few minutes. He remembered his waking moments on the moon almost a half century ago. It was like turning a page in a book. On the first page was a pristine city, on the next, a long dead facility. He sincerely hoped that when he opened his eyes this time and stepped to a porthole, he would see Cosmos fatefully pacing Little One.

A thousand feet away, Jimmy stood in the middle of the main deck and looked up through the *window to the cosmos*. There was a star field. In it, the target; the destination…Alpha Centauri. It seemed so appropriate that it was the brightest star framed in the window. "We'll be able to find it. It's the brightest one Mr. Faulkner," he mused.

Melvin Faulkner, telemetry, checked his numbers again, and then stood and stepped to the center of the deck to look across the lightyears himself, then he continued on to the porthole that framed Little One. At the porthole, he found several children of the colonists that had found a new sport; signaling ship-to-ship with flashlights; using ancient Morse Code, no less. Now there was a mode of communication that had a long history. Probably the only thing older would be smoke signals. Who knows how long that had lasted.

Melvin watched Little One for several moments with an eye searching for variance. There was none; none at all. The two half-mile-wide, quarter-mile high, man-made mountains were in exact lock-step as they powered into the cosmos. It was amazing what computers, properly programmed, could do. Melvin returned to the bridge, took his seat, next to the new communications trainee, sitting in the jump seat, overlooking the Computer and Communications Console. The kid smiled at him. Melvin then looked downward through the massive windshield at the Solar System. The sun was still dominant. He glanced over at Katy Baylor, Computer Control Officer. She was watching Sol, and waiting. Also *waiting*, with patience...was Juan.

Communications with Earth had soon become, more or less, an information stream. As the speed of the two ships became faster and faster, the signal transit time quickly became cumbersome. Now, the favorite signaling was ship-to-ship. It made the small duel-ship-world seem larger. Mentar, now in his early 90's, after due notice, went to sleep. Brock, some fifteen years Mentar's junior, took command of Little One. Younger than him, looking over his shoulder and memorizing every action, was his young trainee...Yaccavan...also patiently waiting.

Colonel Austin delegated the bridge command to Bruce Wilson, the lead pilot, and set up a prearranged routine of rotating the bridge personnel's sleeping time. He then went to sleep himself. He set his timer on the unit for one year with instructions to ascertain that he was indeed awakened in time to meet with Mentar.

DAN HOLT & MAX HOLT

Chapter 20

The Exchange

Mentar City, Earth

The colonists on Earth, the giants, were busy about settling in as new citizens of planet Earth. As the days, weeks, and months rolled by, life slowly became routine. Schools were set up for the youth. Interaction with the *little ones,* to learn each other's lifeways, was treated as an elective in the schools on both sides of the experience. The *little ones* never tired of hearing about Zannia, with its pedestal cities and near planet-wide rain forests. Descriptions of its exotic birds with wingspans of twelve to even twenty feet. They loved hearing about its herds of animals, miles square, roaming through the trees grazing on the undergrowth. A planet, relieved of its burden of indiscriminate stewardship, had come back strong.

Kaavar City, Zannia

Kronos stood on the empty launching pad at Zannia's Spaceport. Mentar had initiated construction of another landing pad to accommodate the in-transit Cosmos that would arrive with Little One. Kronos was here to check on its progress. He looked to the west. A road leading away from the spaceport, winding through two miles of plush rain forest, led to Little One Village; a town scaled down seven times to accommodate the arriving colonists from Earth. Kronos chose to take an afternoon stroll down the road to view Little One Village one more time before it would be occupied by *little ones*; friends from afar.

As he turned to go, a bright flash caught his eye. A lone meteor was transiting the star system, the temporary glow caused by the slight brush with Zannia's atmosphere. It had bounced off and was headed out into deep space. Meteors had always come in showers, as he remembered. But, considering it an anomaly, he dismissed it and headed back to his office.

Chapter 21

In Transit

Year Two

Mentar, aboard Little One, opened his eyes, took a deep breath, and made the decision to remain lying on his back for a few minutes. He heard the two doctors conversing next to his animation unit. They had noted his awakening and were waiting for his gesture to sit up. Mentar soon accommodated them. He felt fine. What a wonderful addition to Zannia's starship. He had just crossed millions of miles without growing older or consuming a sizable amount of provisions. The two doctors did their routine, were satisfied, and left. Mentar got up, took care of his basic needs and headed for the bridge.

Only a thousand feet away, through open space, Jimmy rubbed his face and then tried to sit up. He felt the doctor's stethoscope on his chest and laid back down. The doctor removed it and smiled. "Sounds good."

"A year has gone by?"

"Yes, sir."

Colonel Austin stood, remained in place for a moment, and then looked at the doctor. "No wonder I'm hungry."

151

With that, he headed for the bridge. Upon arrival, he keyed the ship-to-ship communications. Little One's Communications Center answered.

"Yes, sir?"

"Is Mentar awake?"

"Yes, sir. A couple of hours, ago."

"Get him on the horn for me."

"Hello, Colonel, how was your first sleep period?" Mentar said.

"I handled it just fine. I don't feel a year older."

"That's the beauty of it; you're not. I'm having a special meal prepared for me. Why don't you come over and join me; we can talk."

"What are you having?"

"It's a special soup. I had a time getting the recipe. It's the soup the *little ones* served me on the moon forty years, ago. I developed a taste for it. I think we have a measuring cup that will make a fine earthling-size bowl."

"Very funny. I'll be right over."

Jimmy ordered Bobby Ward, a Guppy Crew Chief, to power up his craft for a transfer to Little One. His telemetry team, computer control team, and computer safety systems personnel wanted to accompany him to Little One to confer with their counterparts. Guppy 1, once powered up, would automatically match the acceleration of Cosmos, since it was going the same speed as the Mother Ship, as it sat inside the hangar. They just needed to sync the rotor pod settings with the

Mother Ship. Jimmy then added a fraction of extra power to rise from the hangar-bay deck and exit from Cosmos and slowly make the thousand-foot journey to Little One.

One had to rely on instruments to know of the twin starships' movement through space. The vast distances in the fabric of space made the ships appear to be sitting still in the star-speckled void, as the guppy proceeded across the gap separating the two vessels.

Jimmy saw the size of Little One slowly increasing in his front window. The hangar bay had been depressurized and opened to allow their entry. Pressure-suited giants stood ready to receive them and secure the guppy inside. He glanced at the Instrument Panel to confirm the Doppler Radar was set to slow the craft within ten feet of the hangar bay.

Suddenly, the Master Warning Alarm sounded and red lights flashed everywhere.

Jimmy looked back out the front window. Little One had disappeared! Nothing! Empty Space!

"What the...?"

Bobby jumped to the panel and switched to the Rear-View Monitor. He had to yell to be heard over the loud piercing alarm.

"COLONEL! COSMOS HAS DISAPPEARED!"

Jimmy checked the screen...empty space! He yelled back, "WHAT...what was the failure? All instrument readings are normal!"

"I don't know, sir! It seems like they just slipped out of view, like they put on the brakes, or something."

The other teams accompanying them to Little One instinctively tightened their belts. Jimmy double-checked the console…all readings were still normal.

Bobby tapped his finger on the **Distance to Object** gauge. It should have been reading about **50 YARDS**. Instead, it read **52,000 YARDS,** and the numbers were climbing; spinning like a top.

"The failure has got to be on Cosmos," Bobby shouted. "Our Master Warning System is slaved to theirs. If one vessel has a failure, both alarms go off. Something must have stopped their acceleration. And since Little One is electronically connected to Cosmos, both ships would react the same to any failure. The problem could be on Little One."

"Could be. Either way, we've got to get this guppy stopped. Prepare for *zero-g*!" Colonel Austin ordered.

Bobby hurried to the Maintenance Panel to make the adjustments. The two of them buckled up, while the others checked their safety belts. The Colonel called out to Bobby, "MUTE THE ALARMS!"

Bobby reached and muted the ear-piercing alarm.

"Okay, turn on the side-viewer!"

Bobby made the selection on the Viewer System panel, looking in the direction toward Earth. He selected **MAGNIFY**. In the distance, both massive space craft were just dots on the screen; getting smaller every second.

Jimmy looked around at his passengers. "Everybody, check your belts; going to weightlessness." He hesitated; "On my mark, in five seconds… four…three…two…one; "MARK!"

The rotor pods were switched to *zero-thrust*. Some on the teams had brought briefcases and other small items that had to be grabbed to keep them from floating around the cabin.

Bobby took the next required action. "Rotation started."

Jimmy watched the front viewer, as the guppy completed its slow 180. The *dots*, the only things that could sustain their lives in this forbidding volume of empty space, were registering as tiny little specks on the screen; almost out of sight.

"Engage power," the colonel said.

Bobby activated the pods, and gravity returned.

"Give me *three-G's* for thirty seconds. We've got to get Guppy 1 slowed down so they will catch us. Then reduce thrust to *one-quarter-G*. We don't want to go all the way through one of the ships."

Bobby made the adjustment. "Yes, sir...*three G's*...thirty seconds; then *one-quarter-G*."

With the immediate solution in process, Jimmy activated the ship-to-ship link with Cosmos.

"Cosmos, this is Guppy 1."

No response.

"Cosmos, this is Guppy 1, come in, over!"

As Jimmy was about to key a third time, he heard a strained answer. "Yeah...uh, Colonel...sir...we got a problem here! All of a sudden, we went to *zero-g*...all the rotor pods shut down...uh...all of em! Then, you guys just disappeared out into the distance. We're all floating around over here. Everything not tied down is all over the place!

"Well, I got the Guppy turned around and decelerating back to your velocity. You and Little One will catch us in a few minutes. What happened?! Did you have an impact?

"No, sir, no impact. Everything just came to a halt. Since we are linked with Little One, it stopped, too. We activated a Maintenance Emergency—they're checking. They should have an idea any time…"

Colonel Austin heard a muffled voice.

"Wait, sir, I'm getting something from Maintenance."

More muffled conversation.

"OK, sir, Maintenance says all of Cosmos' systems are fine…no problems here, except stuff is floating everywhere. The problem seems to be on Little One. We stopped accelerating because they did. The link caused us to stay with them." Another pause. "Sir, Mentar is coming on the line for a three-way conversation."

Mentar spoke in his usual calm voice. "Colonel, we seem to have had a total failure of our Magnetic Flux Generator System. Regulator number 17, on the housing area deck, overheated and then failed completely. When it went off-line, all others shut down."

Jimmy's eyes widened. "That means…"

"Yes, we are coasting at almost 170 million miles an hour; one-quarter light-speed, without hull protection. Fortunately, Cosmos still has hull protection. If we can't get this fixed shortly, we'll move everybody to Cosmos and put half of them to sleep."

Jimmy agreed. "Good idea." He paused, "Okay, I've got the guppy turned around and decelerating; we will be there in a few minutes. Make sure your hangar deck is open for me."

"We'll be ready."

Mentar's declaration of Maintenance Emergency had his crew, maintenance team, and security personnel donning their magnetic boots, stored in their lockers. Moving around the ship would be difficult enough without having to deal with weightlessness.

When Jimmy finally had the two ships in visual contact he eased up to the hangar door and went totally weightless. He didn't want to fly into the hangar with so much debris floating around. The young giants inside the hangar, suited and ready, used their articulated-armed grappling hooks to reach out and bring the guppy inside and secure it with tie-downs.

Jimmy looked out the window to see the flurry of activity. Most of Little One's available crew were suiting up in magnetic boots. Others were using hand-held thrusters to chase down the few tools and equipment floating and bouncing off walls and support beams. He was startled when a footlocker-sized metal box, probably a toolbox, bounced off the guppy's windshield and tumbled toward the hangar wall. The guppy's occupants had to be patient until the giants could get things under control, close the hangar door and then pressurize, so they could exit. No one in the hangar noticed what the toolbox hit when it impacted the hangar wall.

A thousand feet away, Cosmos was also in chaos. When the rotor pods kicked off-line, the highly-trained crews of the DOEs had been in their Ready Room, near their hangar. It was a daily routine to train the new recruits on the mission. The young pilots needed to be ready for whatever was required to keep Cosmos safe.

As they all became weightless, they knew what to do; they had trained for it. They reached out to each other and began pushing off and bouncing until they could grab some structural part of the ship. Then, they went hand-over-hand to their aircraft and acquired the pistol-grip thrusters stored there. Using the thrusters, each went to his assigned part of the ship, as instructed by the Emergency Plan. The ship's Maintenance Team also had retrieved their thrusters and were headed to their assigned areas.

As was the case in Little One, most of Cosmos' inhabitants were floating, out of control. Some of the younger children were crying, while many teenagers were already making it into a game. They were pushing off walls, doing acrobatics, and even playing *chicken*, by pushing off opposite walls, directly at each other.

The emergency responders, under control with their thrusters, began the process of first collecting the free-floating fellow travelers and then turning their attention to the loose objects and equipment that might cause damage when gravity was restored. They knew it could be a long process, depending on how long the Magnetic Flux Generator was down.

Back on Little One, the hangar bay door was finally closed and secured and the hangar was pressurized. Before Jimmy and his crew exited the guppy into the hangar, they donned their magnetic boots from the guppy's maintenance locker. With great effort, they made their way toward mid-ship and met up with Mentar on the Bridge. They went over all the Alarm Readings and both agreed that it was only the Magnetic Flux System that had failed. Mentar instructed his crew to speak English so Jimmy and his crew would understand everything.

Jimmy looked at Mentar. "Any idea what caused Regulator Number 17 to overheat and fail?"

"None, yet. We're checking at the location."

Momentarily, Little One's internal communications link activated. The maintenance team had reached Magnetic Flux Regulator Number 17.

"Mentar."

"Yes. I am here…go ahead, what did you find?"

There was hesitation. "Uh…I'm not quite sure what this is."

"Describe it."

"Yes, sir…uh, the ventilation port providing airflow into the regulator is clogged with some sort of sticky substance. Maybe you should come take a look."

"Okay, Colonel Austin is here. We are on our way." He looked around at the young communications trainee, "Yaccavan, monitor the Intercom."

The young giant just stared straight ahead. "Yes, sir, Mentar."

When Little One had been built decades ago, by a combined workforce of giants and little ones, both types of access ladders and entry portals were installed, to accommodate their different body sizes. Those accommodations would come in handy at this point.

Mentar and Jimmy, with several others in tow, made their way through several corridors and up a series of ladders to the deck where the giants' living quarters were located. The going was slow in magnetic boots. They had to take time to move obstructions that had floated into doorways during the weightlessness.

Arriving at the problem regulator, the maintenance team stepped aside to let Mentar and Jimmy have a look. The team chief leaned in close to them and said: "I can't be sure, but we may have a saboteur on board."

The two leaders looked at each other. A chill ran down Jimmy's spine. He had considered the possibility but hadn't given it much serious thought. As they looked closely, they could see that the opening to the ventilation pipe into the Regulator, about the size of a soft ball, was completely clogged with a greyish-looking soft, almost gooey, substance. Mentar buried a finger into the stuff and pulled out a hunk. He looked at Jimmy. "Do you know what it is?"

As Mentar held the gooey stuff up, Jimmy smelled a familiar odor. He sniffed again then looked around at his Crew Chief. "Bobby, smell this."

Bobby took a whiff. "I'll be damned."

Mentar raised his eyebrows. "What?"

Jimmy glanced to his left as a small piece of yellow paper affixed to aluminum foil floated by. He looked back at Mentar. "My friend, I know what caused the failure. Wrigley's Juicy Fruit chewing gun. An Earth treat. It must have taken 50 packs for a wad that size.

Mentar looked at him and then back to the gooey substance on his finger. He switched the 'wad' to his left hand, then with his right hand clear, Mentar reached into the air duct and pulled out the rest of the gum, clearing the obstruction. He reset the air flow system fans. A few minutes later a light on the unit turned from red to green. Mentar turned to Maintenance. "Coordinate with Cosmos and do a 90 second soft power-up to *1-G*."

Mentar looked again at the gum in his hand "I remember this now. We forbade our youth from partaking of such Earth treats...it is bad for their teeth and their metabolism. Someone may well be trying to interrupt our mission. Does anybody know how it got here? This...uh...forbidden treat could have caused the destruction of our ship!"

"Yes, I do," came from near one of the support beams. A female giant was holding herself down to the floor with an arm around the beam. With her other hand, she had an uncomfortable grip on the hand of a young giant...a teenager. "Here is the culprit." She pulled him around her and out in front of Mentar. "Tell him."

The young giant was nervous. "Yes, sir, Mentar...the earth-gum belongs to me."

Mentar approached to within inches of the youngster's face. "WHY...did you sabotage this unit with it?!"

Fearfully he said, "Sir, I didn't know it would mess up the ship. I knew the earth-gum was against our rules, but...but, I had tried it on Earth, and it just tasted so good. A *little one* my age got it for me and I've had it hidden since we launched, looking for a chance to chew it. Today, I finished my school work early so I sneaked out here alone to finally enjoy the gum. I had to open all the packages to make a wad big enough to chew. But, it wasn't long before a maintenance tech came through. I knew if he caught me he would tell. So, I had to get rid of it. This opening seemed like the best place at the moment. I was going to come back and get it as soon as he was gone. But, all of a sudden, everything went crazy; objects were floating everywhere. I got scared, so I went and told my teacher. I'm really sorry"

All eyes went to Mentar, wondering how he would handle such a mundane task as discipline for a wayward youth. After all, youths throughout history had struggled with decisions concerning their desires and right and wrong, as they traversed the complicated path toward adulthood. Mentar paused a moment.

"Restrict him to the living spaces and school until further notice. Talk to his parents for me. Also, develop classroom instruction for all students, teaching them about the dangers of accessing or damaging ship's systems. This incident will be a perfect time to better guarantee a safe journey. The ship has been running so smoothly, we have gotten sloppy and careless. We had a lot of floating debris.

"Yes, Mentar." The teacher nodded her head and floated away, from beam to beam, with her *prisoner* in tow.

As everyone watched, Mentar lifted his finger, with the wad of gum, to his nose and took a breath. "Juicy Fruit, huh?" He cut his eyes at Jimmy, allowing a tiny momentary smile to cross his lips. "It does smell good."

In short order, they felt the soft start underway. The few small items still airborne settled to the floor to be collected by the near 100% participation in cleanup.

Mentar and Jimmy transmitted to their maintenance offices, instructions to fabricate mesh screens to be affixed to the ventilation openings on all Magnetic Flux Regulators. The discussions, *"We should have thought of that before,"* were short lived.

The citizens of the duo of starships had just gotten a stark reminder that you cannot take artificial gravity for granted. The real stuff belonged the planets. They could not roam around the cosmos, but they had an exclusive on a never-interrupted-attraction, GRAVITY, tailored for each individual, to theirs and the planet's body weight.

Finally, hours late, Jimmy and Mentar enjoyed a meal together. They reviewed the journey to Zannia so far, and set an itinerary for the remainder of the transit to Alpha Centauri. Crewmembers, especially

Maintenance, would stay on a renewed state of alert, checking and double-checking all critical systems.

Generally, the two leaders agreed to their schedule: it was sleep a year, wake a month, then repeat until the two suns were shining in the window. They also issued orders to be awakened immediately if there was another problem, of any kind.

A few minutes into the leaders' discussions, a courier from maintenance approached Mentar and spoke in *Moon.* Jimmy had learned the language but the courier spoke so quickly that the only word Jimmy understood was, *shuttle.* Mentar jumped up from the table and looked at Jimmy. "Follow me!" he said.

In a few minutes, they were in Little One's hangar bay. All maintenance personnel and Bay Operators had gathered and seemed to be in a chaotic discussion. "English! Speak English!" Mentar demanded. "I want Colonel Austin to hear this!"

He approached the Hangar Operations Chief, whose darkened giant face was somewhat ashen. If Jimmy had ever seen a hint of anger on Mentar's face; this was it.

"A shuttle?! You lost a shuttle?! How could this happen?!"

Jimmy looked around. Earlier, during weightlessness, when the giants had grappled the guppy into the hangar, he remembered them having to move his craft around one of the giants' shuttles, that was partially blocking the air lock door. The guppy was still there but the large shuttle was gone. Lying at the base of the wall, near where the missing shuttle had been moored, was the large metal tool box that had bounced off his shuttle during his arrival in the hangar.

The Hangar Chief composed himself. "Mentar, you are most aware of the chaos we have just gone through, due to this failure. When Colonel Austin's craft was grappled into the hangar, the tool box you see near that wall, bounced off his guppy and impacted the wall above the shuttle. The Automatic Tiedown Release switches for all shuttles are installed there. Everyone in the hangar was distracted by the emergency and failed to notice that the moorings on Shuttle Number Five..."

"Shuttle Five?! That's my shuttle!"

"Yes, sir. It took a while to get the loose debris under control, so the crew could close the hangar door and pressurize the bay for Colonel Austin and his crew. The only explanation I have is that your shuttle slowly and silently drifted outside. The only crewmen left to secure the hangar were trainees and not aware of how the shuttles were arranged. No one noticed the shuttle was missing until the Duty Crew returned to the hangar. By then, you had reengaged the pods and accelerated away." He paused. "Is it possible to reverse course and retrieve it?"

Mentar shook his head. "No, that would be a long shot. If the shuttle was drifting sideways as it exited the door, it is still drifting sideways, out of our flight path. Even if we went back, there's no guarantee that our sensors will pick up its location." He looked at Jimmy. "What do you think?"

DAN HOLT & MAX HOLT

"I agree with Mentar. Besides, to go back we will have to take the ships through weightlessness twice more. Also, it would probably take a search pattern, all the while, both ships would be weightless. That would be quite stressful, especially for the families. I know you regret losing a shuttle, but I think it's better to take the loss—and learn from it."

Mentar thoughtfully nodded and turned to the Hangar Chief. "Fabricate some protective covers for all remaining switches, so a repeat will be less likely. And, find a way to secure all tool boxes, except the ones being actively used."

"Yes, sir."

While returning to dinner, Jimmy said, "Well, looks like there is another chunk of space debris out there now. What do you think will happen to it?"

"It's drifting at about one-fourth light speed, off our direct course. In a few years, it will bypass Zannia by millions of miles and disappear into the galaxy. Of course, without hull protection it could also be destroyed long before the galaxy welcomes it."

Jimmy smiled, "Maybe some other race will find it and make it their flag ship. Was there anything important inside?"

"Not really, just a duplicate set of detailed navigation plans for ships approaching Zannia, and," he smiled, "a copy of the recipe for my soup."

Jimmy chuckled, "Not to worry, our chef can make it from memory."

Two hours later, Colonel Austin and company flew back to Cosmos. Jimmy toured the ship, touching base with all the departments. The daily activity on board had taken back on a routine atmosphere. School for the young, the daily tending aspects of the family units, and the input of transmissions from Earth. Life aboard Cosmos went on, maintaining the life-cycle of Zannia. Power down at night, power up at dawn, by the clock.

Year Three

It seemed that year-three sneaked up on Cosmos rather quickly. Perhaps a compliment on the general atmosphere of a starship hurling through space at an ever-increasing velocity. The two commanders were awakened for their ritual meal and meetings. The occupants of the starships had grown to accept the relative size of their world for the next six years and were enjoying the day-to-day living. Once in a while, there were mishaps here and there; minor ones...nothing like the Magnetic Flux Regulator failure.

But, it was the little *occurrences* that made life onboard interesting. One of the little girls, a tom-boy-type, was playing in a parked R-bot and fell off it, skinning her knee. Everyone in Medical had to have a look before dressing it. The *wounded* was delighted by how much attention you could get with a minor scrape. Seven hugs were included. The medical staff's normal routine was annual physicals and routine preventive medicine. They didn't *want* any injuries onboard, but they took the opportunity to actually practice the emergency skills they had learned.

The engine room of Cosmos, staffed by five technicians, was humming a single-pitched song, times a hundred and fifty rotor pods. Thirty more sat mute in the tool room, ready to get involved. The techs had a routine to do an electronic check three times a day, then, once a day, a team of two would walk among the rotor pods as a precaution just to know that everything was well. Today, it was Cecil and Byron's turn to take the stroll. They started the three-mile route that would take them within a visual and ear-shot of all the running rotor pods.

Just over a year after the Juicy Fruit incident, they were conducting their routine check of the ship's propulsion system. A mile into the zig-zag inspection path of the engine room, they heard an intermittent clicking sound. They froze in their tracks and listened intently. For a couple of minutes, all was quiet. Then it occurred again; a clicking sound for about ten seconds, a pause, then a clicking sound again for about another ten seconds. Cecil reached up to his mic, clipped to his collar, keyed it, and notified the Maintenance Chief. He gave the number of the nearest rotor pod and then started searching from rotor pod to rotor pod, suspecting that one of them was developing a problem. The Maintenance Chief boarded his R-bot and headed for the designated rotor pod.

The two maintenance personnel searched in an ever-widening circle around the spot where they first heard the clicking sound. Minutes later, they stepped around a rotor pod, mounted next to the wall of the ship, and there sat Jeremy Shelton, 10 years old, with a fresh, half eaten, tomato in one hand and a salt shaker in the other. The *zero-g* shaker had a magnetic base and a spring-loaded cylinder inside that would not allow dispensing unless it was being shaken.

When Jeremy looked up at the two technicians, his mouth fell open. He closed it, finished chewing the bite and swallowed. Byron cradled his hands on his hips and looked down at the ten-year-old. "What are you doing?"

"Eating a tomato," Jeremy said and held it up.

The Chief arrived, looked at the two maintenance techs, then noticed Jeremy sitting with his back against the wall, looking from face to face.

"Who are you?" the chief said.

"Jeremy."

"Jeremy who?"

"Jeremy Shelton."

"What are you doing here?'

"Eating a tomato," Jeremy said and held it up again.

"Does your mother know you are here?"

Jeremy shook his head.

"Come with me, young man." The techs and Jeremy boarded the transport and headed back to the Maintenance Office. Jeremy watched the Chief work the controls of the R-bot.

"Can I drive it?"

"Not today, you're in trouble; we've got to go call your mother."

"She's nice."

"Lucky for you."

While they were waiting for Jeremy's mother, the Maintenance Department allowed Jeremy to finish the tomato. The chief's curiosity peaked. "How did you get that tomato out of hydroponics?"

"The watering guy;" Jeremy responded, "the man that works the watering system has a friend. She comes to see him every day. I snuck in, got it, and came back out while they are talking."

"Clever."

As Jeremy's mother led him up the stairs back to the main deck of Cosmos, Jeremy knew that he was in trouble, however, he knew that the *court* would be fair.

Had anyone been keeping a log, Jeremy Shelton would hold the record for being the only youth onboard that was actually grounded for a full month.

Six weeks later, young Shelton showed up at the maintenance door of the engine room.

"Well, hello, Jeremy," the chief said. "You finally got out of jail, huh."

"My mother said I could come and see you for a few minutes. I was wondering how my favorite rotor pod is doing?"

"Favorite?"

"Yeah. The one by the wall."

"Jeremy, all the rotor pods are the same."

"No, sir. Mine is different."

The Chief leaned back in his chair and eyed Jeremy, pausing for a moment. "How? Show me."

They mounted the R-bot. The chief steered it out into the aisle, then moved to the other seat and gestured for Jeremy to get behind the wheel. Jeremy carefully engaged the throttle pedal and steered the machine down the aisle for several hundred feet, then stopped. The chief took the driver's seat and drove the R-bot to the spot where Jeremy had been found.

"It's that one," Jeremy said, pointing to the pod closest to the wall.

"It's the same." The chief said, opening his hands.

Jeremy disembarked the vehicle and stepped over to another rotor pod across the aisle. "Listen to this one," Jeremy said and placed his ear to the pod's outer shell.

The Chief humored him and listened to the hum he'd heard thousands of times. The ten-year-old stepped to the next and did the same. The chief complied.

"Now," Jeremy said. "Listen to mine."

The Chief placed his ear to the shell of the pod and listened. His well-trained ear picked up the lower pitch of the hum instantly. He jerked upright, then placed the other ear to the rotor pod. The hum was definitely lower in pitch than the other two. He hurriedly stepped over to the R-bot, opened the tool box mounted across the back, picked up a specially designed Magnetclamp Vibration Detector, and then stepped back to the rotor pod and clamped it to the outer shell. He turned on the readout. The needle was hovering between green and yellow on the status scale. He turned the sensitivity to maximum and looked again. The needle had gone to the middle of yellow.

"Come on," he said to Jeremy. He then put the tool back into the toolbox and headed back to the Maintenance Office. He sat down in his chair and keyed the intercom to the bridge. "Colonel Austin?"

"Go ahead, Chief."

"Colonel, could you come to the engine room for a moment."

Colonel Austin's eyes went to the twenty-four-inch diameter display of the one hundred and fifty rotor pod status lights on the ship's console. All were green. "On my way," he said.

The Chief introduced the colonel to Jeremy Shelton and related the episode and the subsequent readout to the colonel. Colonel Austin approved shutting down the rotor pod and replacing it from the backups, and then requested a report following the investigation of the anomaly. He turned to Jeremy. "Good job, young man. Are you training on the rotor pods?"

"He will be," the Chief interjected.

Colonel Austin nodded then returned to the bridge.

The chief turned to Jeremy: "When you finish college, I want you on my team."

"I'll be working on rotor pods?"

"All the time."

"Aw—right!"

The chief watched Jeremy ascend the stairs back up to the main deck. He smiled. There seemed to be a special air about him. The chief got up from his desk, walked out among the rotor pods, and listened to a couple of them. They were both right on key; the key of **D**. The hum exactly matched the key of an ancient recording the chief kept in his personal belongings. An artist of old, with a pure voice, sang *Kiss an Angel Good Morning*, in the key of **D,** a recording that the chief had heard privately many times. The chief laid his hand on one of the rotor pods. It was an angel; they all were; a band of angels that were carrying Cosmos to the stars. He looked around, then kissed it, and whispered: "Good morning."

He assembled a team and they made their way to Rotor Pod #39.

A week later, a report was sent to the bridge, to Colonel Austin, concerning rotor pod #39. The mechanism inside was missing a spacer-washer on one of the magnet alignment screws of the vertical rotor. The spacer weighed less than two grams. The experts assessed that the missing part was not enough to disable the rotor pod nor cause danger. However, the minute vibration would shorten the life of the rotor pod bearings by some .001%. No one knew how much run-time that would be, since no rotor pod had ever failed due to old age.

The Chief sought out Jeremy and gave him one of the shiny rotor pod spacers. He explained to Jeremy that now, his rotor pod would run as fast as the rest of them. Jeremy put the spacer on a string and wore it around his neck. When his friends would ask about it. He would respond: "It's a special part that makes rotor pods run faster."

Chapter 22

The Comet

Six months past the half-way point

As the miles rolled by, the day and night routine of Cosmos and Little One was adjusted to their destination: Zannia. The ships were now decelerating. Television was being received from Earth. It occupied many on board with schooling. A dedicated educational channel was faithfully beamed from Earth toward the ships and Zannia. Regular television entertainment filled in between the educational episodes.

Javienne and his band performed monthly with his concerts transmitted to Cosmos as well. Life aboard the mile-wide, combined, portable city became routine as the 300 rotor pods continued to do what they were born to do.

Then, half way through year number five; a call came from Navigation.

Bruce, Cosmos' pilot, answered the intercom. "Go ahead."

"Bridge, we have a comet, about a mile in diameter, pacing us off the starboard bow."

Bruce looked out the windshield off to the right. He saw a fuzzy pin dot. He watched it for a moment. "How far away?"

"Right now, it's a little over three thousand miles from us. However, based on our readings, it will cross our flight path about a hundred thousand miles ahead of us."

"That's a long way. Isn't it a safe clearance?"

"Not at our velocity," Navigation responded. "If it hit anything at all in space, even something small to slow it a little, it could hit us. You better wake up the Colonel."

"Roger," Bruce responded.

Colonel Austin, fully awake, raised up on his elbows. "Another year, huh?"

"No, sir. A little over six months."

Colonel Austin knew what the early wake-up meant. "What happened?" he said as he abruptly sat up, then stood and wavered a little.

The doctors steadied him. "Give yourself a moment for the ole balance-bubble to wake up."

"What happened?" Jimmy repeated.

"There's a comet coming close to the ship. It's as big as these two ships put together."

"Is Mentar awake."

"Yes, sir. The comet is on his side, the starboard side. They picked it up just before we did."

Jimmy hurried to the bridge. Two navigation people were there conferring with the bridge crew. He joined the group.

"Sir," Bruce said, "there's a comet that's going to cross our flight path. Bruce pointed out the windshield, starboard. Colonel Austin located the comet, a fuzzy pin dot, and watched it for a moment, then looked at navigation.

"It's going to cross our flight path about a hundred thousand miles ahead of us. At our velocity, that's close, really close, especially since our velocity is constantly changing and the comet's velocity is always the same."

Jimmy paused a moment, then keyed the intercom: "Captains Snyder and Abbot, to the bridge."

He then keyed the ship-to-ship link. Mentar answered. "Colonel, seems we have a potential obstacle approaching our path. At our convergent speeds, the computer says that it will cross our path about 10 seconds before we get there. Its path seems to be a couple of miles below ours but still, it's very close."

Jimmy looked out the windshield and studied the comet again. He keyed the mic. "Ten seconds, yeah, that's close. Give me a few minutes. I've called our DOE pilots to the bridge to discuss it. I'll keep you on the Monitor Circuit so you can hear."

Moments later, the Captains of the two DOEs arrived. When they saw the Colonel present on the bridge, they became alert. "Yes, sir?"

Colonel Austin stepped close to the windshield and pointed at the tiny fuzzy ball to the right. The two pilots joined him and studied the white dot in the star-speckled void. "What's that," Captain Snyder said.

"It's a comet," navigation said, "about a mile in diameter. It's going to cross our flight path up ahead, in about three hours.

"Is it going to hit us!"

"No, if there's no change in it trajectory. It will cross our flight path a hundred thousand miles ahead of us. At our speed, we will cross that spot about 10 seconds later, although the computers say it will be a little below and well clear before we get there. However, if there's the slightest change, if it hits any obstruction, even a tiny one, it could slow enough to hit us."

From the intercom, a voice, sounding concerned, asked for Bruce. He keyed the system. "Yes, go ahead."

"This is Navigation. We have coordinated with Little One's navigators to determine and confirm the comet's orbit. It will pass through our Solar System again sixteen years and four months from now. Ten years after that, it will pass somewhere near the Alpha Centauri system."

The bridge crew all looked at each other. Momentarily, Colonel Austin keyed the mike. "Is it going to hit Earth?"

Mentar could be heard, under his breath, *"Or, Zannia?"*

"Colonel?"

"Yes."

"Sir, we can't tell if it will hit Earth, however, it will go through the Solar System on a plane that means all the planets and their moons could be targets. There is a possibility that Earth could be impacted. We would have to wait another ten years from now to reanalyze and confirm its exact path."

Jimmy turned to Snyder and Abbott. "Can you land on that thing and push on it; change its orbit?"

"We can try, sir," Snyder said. Abbot nodded.

Jimmy keyed the intercom again. "Navigation."

"Yes, sir?"

"We are going to send the two DOEs over there to land on the comet and try to push on it and change its orbit. What do you think. How much do we need to move it?"

"One moment, sir."

An awkward minute went by. Mentar keyed his mic. "Colonel, your plan sounds logical. But, encourage your pilots to exercise extreme caution; comets can be very unpredictable. We cannot afford to lose one of those special ships, or its very capable crew."

"Noted, Mentar." Colonel Austin turned to Snyder and Abbott. "If you see that the attempt is too risky, return to the ship and we'll alter the trajectory of Little One and Cosmos. We need to alter the comet's orbit if we can."

"We'll take a look, sir."

Navigation responded: "It's a mile in diameter, with average density. If the two DOEs pushed on it at full power for thirty minutes, they should be able to change its trajectory about two centimeters. The computer says it would then miss the earth by at least a quarter-million miles."

Mentar keyed in. "What about Zannia?"

Navigation paused. "The change would cause it to miss your system by at least a million."

Captain Snyder looked at his fellow DOE pilot, then at the colonel. "Smart guys."

"Yeah."

"Okay, we're on it."

The two DOEs approached the comet. They seemed very tiny up beside its bulk. Snyder keyed ship-to-ship with Cosmos. "Colonel, we are approaching the comet. There are several smaller balls of ice flying along with it. I count seven. They are each about the size of a house."

"Oh, boy. They could do some damage. Can you pulverize them?"

"I think so, sir, but there will be some tiny ice-crystals still left."

Mentar keyed in. "That won't be a problem for our magnetic shields."

The Colonel agreed. "Quite right, they will protect us."

There was a pause in conversation as the two DOEs moved into position. Then, they hovered near the tail of the comet. Captain Snyder keyed in. "I'm locked onto the two biggest ice balls, ready to fire."

"Okay, I've got the rest targeted," Abbott reported.

"Fire on my command," Captain Snyder ordered.

The bridge crew became silent, along with the twenty or so people that had formed a semicircle around the bridge. Silence also fell on Little One's bridge.

Momentarily, they heard the command from Snyder. The four cannons roared for thirty seconds, then spun down to silence. The strong recoil of the massive fire-power would have slowed the speed of the DOE, had it not been for the rotor pods' compensation circuitry.

"Piece of cake," Abbott said. "They are expanding mists of snow."

"Colonel," Snyder added, "this cloud of mist will make a magnificent tail for the comet-watchers in the Solar System."

"Yes, Captain, when Earth gets the message, I can see the headlines. LITTLE ONE COMET—TAIL PROVIDED BY SNYDER AND ABBOT."

There was scattered laughter among the crews.

Snyder's voice came from the radio again.

"Okay, Colonel, we're approaching the nucleus. It's sizable; about half the size of the comet."

"Good," navigation responded. "It's one of the more stable ones."

"Landing on it now," Snyder radioed.

Moments later the two DOEs, having landed, engaged power toward the center of mass of the comet's nucleus, gradually increasing it to full output.

Each of the DOE pilots spent thirty minutes with their safety harness's tight and their hands over the emergency shutdown control. When the clock timed out, they gradually brought the power to zero thrust, then reversed, relative to their ships, and eased away from the comet.

"How's that?" Snyder radioed.

Navigation responded. "Standby, we need for it to travel about thirty minutes for radar tracking."

"Roger, standing by."

Finally, Navigation radioed, "That's it, you moved it just over two centimeters. It will miss Earth by a quarter million miles and bypass Alpha Centauri completely."

Mentar keyed in. "Excellent, excellent, excellent."

Jimmy agreed. "Good job, gentlemen, come on home."

"We're on our way."

Most occupants of both ships had been watching the DOE activity out every available window. Thirty minutes later, all had an amazing close-up view of a comet, as it crossed their path out front and below their ships.

Chapter 23

The Object

Colonel Austin took a large spoonful of soup from the measuring cup Mentar had provided. It was their sixth *wake-up* meal together, as usual, on Little One. He had acquired a taste for Mentar's favorite dish, born out of necessity on the moon, over 40 years ago. Over the years, it had found its way into restaurant menus on both worlds...MENTAR SOUP; small, medium & large.

Following the meal, they had the usual routine briefings from all departments on both ships. All had been well during their *sleep*, save for a few minor maintenance issues and some relationship issues, all handled by the awake crews.

During some small talk, about life in general and some general plans to help settle the colonists on Zannia, Jimmy shared one observation; that there had been several reports during the last year, of late-night communicating from ship-to-ship, using the old Morse Code, with flashlights. None of the kids admitted to having been awake at those hours. Jimmy said, "It seems to be happening while Juan and Yaccavan are on Communications Duty. Let's ask them to start watching out the window during those hours; maybe they can catch whoever is doing it."

Mentar agreed. He said, "It is interesting to see all of the things the young can devise to amuse

183

themselves. That's one thing our young are learning from yours…how to play. We have noticed that those in our school seem to have a more creative approach to learning since interacting with *little one* children. Even Menvaar seems happier since, during cross-culture training, some of your youth taught him a game they play in Cosmos' Shuttle Hangar. I believe it is called basketball. He said he would like to teach it to the youth on Zannia. Of course, the size of the ball and net will have to change. But, that's a good thing we have picked up from your culture."

Jimmy agreed. "Our culture has also learned from yours. I like the way our children have learned to be more serious about how to better apply what they are learning. A definite positive transference from your culture."

Mentar smiled. "Well, my friend, it seems we are still linked from 50,000 years ago. But I still have much to learn. Your children enjoy playing but I have also noticed that your adults have many recreational pursuits that I would categorize as *playing*."

Jimmy nodded, "Yes, that's true. For instance, I have enjoyed snow skiing since I was a child…I never get tired of it. But, I'm guessing there aren't too many ski resorts on Zannia…right?"

Mentar shook his head. "I have seen that activity on your television but we have no such activity on Zannia, although we do have snow in our polar regions. We have never even considered it as something we would enjoy."

There was a lull in the conversation.

Finally, Jimmy asked, "Mentar, I have been curious about the Module you and Kavientar recovered from the moon. Have you done any further analysis on it?"

"Yes. Kavientar has led my best onboard experts, trying to make some sense of its significance. All they found was some vague references in our History Archives, about artifacts left behind by our ancient ancestors. But, we have no real information about any such ancestors, apart from the ones we can trace back for many millennia. At some point in our history, the records just disappear. It's almost like…uh…we just dropped out of the sky."

"Well, I wish you, and him, luck in the search for your past. After all, we were able to determine ours."

Mentar's *knowing* smile was refreshing.

Jimmy continued. "Right now, I need to get back and update my Ship's Log and get to know my people again."

"Yes, I must do the same."

Two weeks later, Kavientar was at the helm of Little one, coordinating with Bruce on Cosmos, confirming the settings for their last course adjustment before the final leg to Zannia. The Radar Operator switched to the long-distance system, reaching a million miles out, checking for any debris that could be in their path. These routine sweeps during course changes never found anything; space was indeed a void. But, this time was different. The yellow caution light began flashing on his console. The blip on the screen was so tiny that

185

he almost couldn't see it. For a moment, he doubted it was there. Even though the light was flashing, he brushed across the screen to confirm it was not a speck of dust that had floated in. He keyed his personal link to Cosmos' Radar Operator and asked if he saw it, too.

"Yeah," came the reply. "I was about to call you. Both systems can't be wrong. What do you make of it."

The giant on Little One hesitated. "I'm not sure. Let's report it."

Mentar immediately opened a link to Jimmy.

"Colonel, my radar is showing an object about three-quarters of a million miles out. If it stays on its course, it should miss us by half that distance."

"Yes, Mentar, I am reading the same here. Do you think it is another comet, or maybe a meteor?"

Kavientar was shaking his head. "I don't think it's a comet. Our scanners can't seem to detect its make-up. How about yours, Colonel?"

Jimmy looked at his Radar department; the operator was shaking his head. He keyed his mic again. "No, we don't have a good reading either. But, at its current velocity, it should pass off the port side, a least a couple of hundred thousand miles out. It shouldn't be a concern."

"Agreed."

Both commanders were beginning their entries into their Ship's Logs, about the object, when both radar systems activated their RED ALERTS, with the audible alarms and red lights flashing…the object was changing course.

Cosmos saw it first.

"COLONEL…the object is changing course!"

As Jimmy stared at the screen, Mentar keyed in, "Our system shows a course change as well." He hesitated. "Colonel…it is changing course…toward us."

There was silence on both bridges as both radar crews tried to assess the situation. Cosmos' crew confirmed it. Bruce looked up at Jimmy. "Sir, that thing is tracking us…unless we do something, it's going to hit us!"

Jimmy said, "What *is* that thing, an alien ship?" Then he thought. "Uh…Mentar, could it be that Zannia has sent someone out to escort us back to the planet."

"Quite impossible, Colonel. Little One is the only rotor-pod-equipped craft we have that could make such a course change in open space, at that speed. No, it is definitely not from Zannia."

Cosmos' radar chief interrupted. "Sir, we just did another scan. It is a metal object, about the size of an R-bot. It is headed right for us, and it is…ah…wait…this can't be…"

Little One's operator picked up the report. "Yes, Cosmos, you are right…the object is slowing.

Another voice entered the conversation. It was the Little One Facilities Chief, responsible for all storage spaces. "Mentar, we have a possible emergency in Storage Bay, Alpha 21…"

187

Mentar interrupted, "Not now, we are dealing with an emergency here…the possible collision with a space object."

The Facilities Chief insisted. "Mentar, I have been monitoring your emergency. Do you remember what is stored in Alpha 21?"

Mentar hesitated. "The Module! But what does it have to do with this foreign object?"

"I'm not sure, sir, but five minutes ago, uh…the Module turned on…it is glowing."

Pin-drop silence…just the whirring of gyros in the main instrument panel.

"Glowing?"

"Yes. Thirty minutes ago, during the inventory of storage units, one of my personnel noticed the container was warm to the touch. He called me. I opened the container to ensure nothing had harmed or damaged the Module. It was uncomfortably hot to the touch. Five minutes ago, the glass on one end began glowing a bright green. Now it is pulsing; bright and dim, bright and dim."

Little One's radar operator spoke: "Mentar, I'm receiving a signal from the object…in the low megahertz range. I can't detect any intelligence in the signal…it's like nothing I've ever heard before."

Cosmos chimed in. "Yeah, my radar's getting the same signal. The pattern is repeating…like…uh…"

Jimmy looked over. "Like what?"

"It's looking for a response," Mentar said.

"What response…we don't know how to respond."

Mentar looked at Kavientar and keyed the mic. "We don't have to...the Module is responding." He looked at the Radar operator. "Is the object still slowing?"

"Yes, sir. Its path will bring it alongside us; starboard side."

Mentar nodded. "Alpha 21 Storage Unit is on the starboard side."

Soon, the object appeared on the Monitor Screen on each commander's console. It had parked itself alongside Little One, fifty feet away, near the hangar airlock door. It was the size of an R-bot, cylindrical, and blunt on both ends. Green lights circled one end and were flashing to the rhythm of the signal Radar had received.

Mentar directed a Scanning Team to the hangar. Before opening the hangar door, the team, in tethered pressure suits, exited through personnel hatch and approached the object, with a biological scanner in hand.

"Mentar, we are sensing no biological signal of any kind around the object. We have checked both ends and there doesn't appear to be any recognizable propulsion system on it. There must be some unknown drive inside.

Mentar hesitated and then keyed in. "Colonel, I am going to have the object brought onboard. We will broadcast the video and audio links to you, so you can watch our progress."

The hangar door was opened and the object was grappled inside. Mentar instructed Facilities to retrieve the Module from Alpha 21 storage and bring it to the hangar bay. As the two mysterious objects were brought closer together, the flash of the lights became faster and faster, until both were glowing constantly. Mentar had the hangar video cameras linked to the ship's primary system, allowing Cosmos to view the proceedings.

Mentar and Kavientar made their way to the hangar to have a closer look. The object appeared to be solid metal, no protrusions, no antenna, no solar panels, no access doors or panels; just an...object. The flashing green lights on one end seemed to be part of the metal. There were markings all around the cylinder but they were so worn that no one could tell if they were identification marking or perhaps a language.

The entire metal surface was deteriorated, as though it had been in space for eons. There were no burn marks or any attaching points, as would be if it had been launched from a spacecraft.

Mentar keyed his mic. "Colonel, I trust you are seeing this. What do you make of the condition of the object?"

Jimmy studied the surface of the object for a moment; he remembered something from his basic space training...Worm Hole Theory.

"Mentar, what do you know about worm holes?"

"Worm holes? Yes, our scientists have always believed that worm holes were a reality, although our culture has no record of ever having verified their existence. But, general space theory has always assumed they exist, as portals to other spiral arms of the galaxy and perhaps to other galaxies.

"Colonel, are you suggesting this object came from somewhere else in the galaxy?"

"No, not necessarily. I'm just sort of…grasping at straws, so to speak."

"Yes, I remember that phrase…you *little ones* seem to use it often. Well, we too are *grasping at straws* as well.

After a lengthy inspection and discussion, Kavientar noticed the outline of a six-inch circle on one end of the object. It was almost indistinguishable; the outline having been mostly worn away. He touched it, and nothing happened. Mentar watched, and then stepped to the other end. A similar circle was there, also well worn. He held his finger two inches above it and then gently touched it. He jerked his hand back as the circle dropped into the object and disappeared to the side, followed by an opening two feet in diameter appearing in the end. Inside the opening, it was smooth, with no other openings. Mentar was looking into a cone-shaped opening, the exact size of the tapered glass end of the Module.

"Bring the Module over here."

Jimmy keyed in. "My friend, I advise caution."

Mentar looked at the camera. "I understand and appreciate your concern, but…I must *know.*"

Kavientar stepped to his side as Mentar stared at the camera and spoke.

"Colonel, uh…Jimmy…my friend…should something, uh, *permanent* befall me, explain to those waiting on Zannia."

"Yes, my friend…I will. But, we have come a long way together…I trust the fates will allow us both to arrive, together."

Mentar smiled and turned his attention back to the mysterious object. He instructed two giants to carry the Module around to the cone-shaped opening in the object. When they got within 10 feet of it, some *force* pulled the Module from their hands, into the cone opening. It seated itself with an audible *thud*. The glowing end of the Module and the lights around the end of the object stopped blinking and then went dark.

There was no sound…all were holding their breath. Just as they were ready to breathe again, lights appeared around the cylinder, on the opposite end and began to blink.

From behind, a giant asked, "What is it doing?"

Kavientar looked at Mentar, then at the group in the hangar. "It's still searching."

Mentar paused. "Carefully, store them together in Alpha 21."

Chapter 24

The Hull Inspection

Everyone was enjoying the party atmosphere. After every *wakeup* on both ships, the giants and *little ones,* who had been asleep, would congregate on one of the ships for a time of refreshment and mutual discussion about life on Zannia and to make plans on how to blend their two societies, once they were settled there.

This *wakeup* gathering was on Cosmos. They were enjoying the music of Little One's favorite band. The band chose this time to debut some of the *little ones'* music they had learned on Earth. They had learned to blend it well with their own music.

With the hull inspection coming up, Juan and Yaccavan saw this as a good time to coordinate some of their *plans*, to challenge the leadership. Juan looked on the merriment with disdain. Some of the grandfather's genes had bled through. Both he and Yaccavan felt that there should be a little demonstration to establish that not everyone has to bow to mindless obedience to some uncaring leader.

Since his discussion with the school principle at age 14, Juan had focused on learning all there was to know about all different models of computer systems. Not only was he the best onboard at coding and programming, he had become an expert computer technician. He could take computers apart and put them back together, almost blindfolded. He could even build a star-drive processor from scratch, the system that provided the navigation instructions to the rotor pods.

He and Yaccavan sneaked away from the party so he could show his giant friend what he had constructed. Juan removed it from his pocket and placed it in the giant's hand. To him, it looked the size of a postage stamp.

Juan had constructed a computer coding device the size of a standard credit card, about a quarter-inch thick. With his authority as a top coder on board, he had *requisitioned* several powerful chip-sized processors from Ship's Supply and sandwiched them between the two acrylic halves. There was a tiny wire sticking out from one end, with a USB connector on the end.

Yaccavan studied it. "What are you going to do with it?"

"I already did it."

"What?"

Juan smiled. "Just wait until our shuttle leaves for the hull inspection and you'll see."

"You mean, you disabled a shuttle?"

"Oh, the shuttle still works, but 10 minutes after it launches, they are going to get a big surprise."

With eyebrows raised, Yaccavan said, "Wait, you're not going to harm the Pilots or kill them, are you?!"

"No! That's too risky. What I have done will just get their attention. It will let the leaders know that they are not completely in charge…not in total control of everything."

"What if the pilots figure it out and fix the problem before the mission is impacted?"

Juan laughed. "There is no way they can find, much less fix, what I have done."

"What about the security patrols, or the security cameras in the hangar bay? Are you sure you weren't seen?"

Juan leaned against a support beam. "I know the schedule of the patrols. And, who do you think programs the control systems for those security cameras?"

Yaccavan smiled. "You do"

"Right."

Colonel Austin was awakened from his seventh cycle in his animation unit. Checked and cleared by the medical department of Cosmos, he headed for the bridge and a current report. Katy, computer control specialist, pointed at the navigation screen; "Zannia,"

The colonel's eyes went to the monitor. A tiny dot had appeared, glistening among the vast star field that was the Milky Way. Beside it on the screen was a very small designation, **ZANNIA**. Katy glanced at the ship's commander. The colonel met her eyes. "How far away?"

Kathy glanced at the screen then back to the colonel. "Four months, four days. The reason we haven't seen it sooner is the fact that it has two suns that shine it away."

Jimmy studied the image. "The count is now two."

"Sir?"

"Alpha Centauri is the second star to harbor life that we know about. The count is now two: Alpha Centauri System and the Solar System. I wonder how many more are out there."

"Colonel," Katy began, "I believe there are more worlds, inhabited worlds, out there than there are grains of sand on the beach. We are located on the outskirts of the galaxy, where the stars are sparse. Closer to the galactic core, many of the stars are much closer to each other; light-weeks, even light-days apart. I believe there are communities of four or five star-systems that routinely interact and visit each other; even engage in trade.

"What a vision," Colonel Austin said. "You are probably right. It's the only thing that makes sense, considering the size of the cosmos."

The Maintenance Chief keyed in on Jimmy's command console. "Yes, Maintenance, go ahead."

"Sir, do you want to launch the shuttle now?"

"A shuttle...what for?"

"It's our turn, to do the Annual Hull Inspection. Little One's shuttle did it last year for both ships...it's our turn."

"Oh...yeah. Yes, follow the standard procedure."

"Yes, sir. They should be ready to launch shortly. I'll coordinate with Little One to keep them in the loop."

The crew of the specially equipped Shuttle, Pilot, Cecil Dray, recruited from the Maxie Gene and Wendy Summer, Copilot, from the MaryLou, and Technician, Keenan Wylie, from Discovery, climbed aboard and started their preflight checklist. They were known as the mix-matched crew with a common goal. They all shared a passion to go to the stars. The Survey Shuttle was one of only two survey-equipped shuttles. Survey One and Survey Two were equipped with the hull scanners, able to *see* inside the metal skin and find any weaknesses caused by the stresses of near-light-speed flight through open space.

The Scanner Operator ran the tests on his computer system…all was well. The Pilots ran the tests on the fight control systems and the Proximity Monitor, the device that warned if the shuttle was wandering outside the protection of the generated field around the mother ship.

The Copilot noticed the tiny rubber cover on the USB Data Input Port was missing.

She tapped the Pilot on the arm and informed him.

He glanced at it. "Write it up when we get back and let Maintenance handle it."

"Okay," she said. "All systems are good to go. Shuttle Control and Safety Systems responding normally."

From behind came, "Scanner Systems, good to go."

The Pilot keyed his radio. "Shuttle Launch Control, Survey One is ready for departure. We will begin the hull scan on the port side of Cosmos and end on the starboard side of Little One. Estimated mission time three hours and twenty minutes."

"Roger, Survey One, Cosmos and Little One will be monitoring your hull status transmissions and your cockpit voice frequency. Let us know if you see anything out of the ordinary. Remember to stay inside the bubble, especially when transiting over to Little One. Have a safe mission."

"Roger Launch Control. We have synchronized with Cosmos' acceleration; ready to release moorings…open the outer doors."

"Roger, opening hangar doors."

The massive hangar doors slowly slid apart. The shuttle hovered outside and then up and over the top of Cosmos toward the port side of the vessel. As they came up over the top, the vast star-field in their path burst into view. The crew held its collective breath. They never tired of the incredibleness that was…*space*. Alpha Centauri was dead center of their windshield. They knew that Zannia, too small to see with the naked eye, was parked nearby, awaiting their arrival, with gravity, atmosphere, and sunshine.

The Pilot turned toward the Copilot, who was staring, wide-eyed. "This is why I took this job. The Jet Jockies back home have no idea what they're missing. At moments like this, you know why the risk is worth it."

"Jet Jockies?" Wendy said. "That term's still hanging on?"

"Yeah, the term **jet** has kinda' evolved into meaning *powerful thrust*, not an actual jet fuel burner. Also, it has a nice ring to it."

The crew nodded, smiled, then forced their attention away from the Milky Way, spread before them, and focused on the hull scan.

Beginning at the rear of Cosmos, the Pilot set the automatic tracking system to lock onto the hull and scan a straight path to the front port side. The system would then do a 180 degree turn and scan the next path toward the rear. Once Cosmos was complete, the Pilot would deactivate the scanner, fly over to Little One, and repeat the procedure.

The Pilot engaged the system and then sat back in his seat. The ship began moving over the surface of the mother ship at about the speed a man would walk. For about the next hour and a half the crew could relax and enjoy the black velvety void ablaze with stars.

Shuttle Control saw the Scan Transmission stop. "Survey One, this is Control. The scan has stopped."

"Yeah, Control, we're checking."

Without warning, the Survey Shuttle rotated its bow perpendicular to the two mother ship's line of flight and engaged power at *1G*. The shuttle accelerated away from Cosmos, getting 32 feet-per-second faster every passing second.

"What are you doing?" Cecil asked his Copilot.

"I didn't execute that maneuver!" Wendy grabbed her controls and attempted to correct. "My controls aren't working!"

Cecil grasped his and selected **Station Keeping** on the Flight Control System. The ship completely ignored his input. Cecil keyed the radio. "Control, we have a problem. The ship's in runaway mode! We have no control! The ship changed course away from Cosmos and engaged power at *1G* and has locked out the manual controls. The AVS Avoidance System has engaged and locked us out. We're accelerating away from you like a bat out of hell!"

Jimmy keyed the intercom; "Shuttle bay, get two guppies powered up!" Then he keyed the radio again. "Cecil, this is Colonel Austin, can you do a total shutdown!? We'll send a guppy to tow you back to Cosmos."

"No, sir. We tried that when we realized we didn't have control. The ship is not responding to any input. Colonel," Cecil added, "we can barely see Cosmos."

"Survey One," Colonel Austin said, "we are dispatching two guppies. They will overtake you, grapple onto your shuttle's rear hard point, overpower your ship, and tow you back home."

The crews of Guppies One and Two, quickly powered up their respective ships and readied them for the rescue of the survey shuttle. They exited the mother ship and zeroed in on the electronically-produced pin dot on their radar screens. They set their acceleration at *3G's* until they were receiving a real return from the growing image on the radar screen. At that point, the pilots reduced speed to *2G's*, and then, when there was a visual sighting, throttled back to *one-*

point-one G. Two of the crewmembers were suited and ready to make the connection with the towing equipment.

Juan Valencia, watching the drama unfold from shuttle control, looked at the floor momentarily. His face was drawn and ashen where he thought there would be a smile. He knew that when they recovered the shuttle and had it safely back in Cosmos, they were going to ask him to examine the shuttle's computers and report.

Keenan Wylie, watching the rear-view monitor of Survey One, took a breath when the dot, that was Cosmos and Little One, disappeared. He stared at the blank screen for a moment, and then looked out the windshield at the velvety black star-speckled void. A deep sense of loneliness gripped him.

Survey One's captain glanced at him. "They're coming. Let's make sure all loose items are secured. When they grapple onto us and start slowing our velocity, that rotor pod is going to increase its output, trying to maintain *1G*. When they force this ship to reverse course, it will be screaming at a full *10 G's* We've got to be ready for anything."

Keenan looked back at the rear-view monitor again. A dot had appeared in the middle of it, gradually growing. It was taller than it was wide and had two half-circles on each side. "What's that?" he said hopefully.

"That, my friend," Cecil said, "is the nose of a guppy; beautiful isn't it?"

"Cosmos, this is Guppy One, we have Survey One in sight. She's about a mile ahead."

"Roger, Guppy One. Lock onto it and bring…"

"Colonel," the engine room technician interrupted, "a reminder sir. When Guppy One gets within a hundred feet of Survey One, it must keep its closing speed under 14 feet-per-second. Any faster, and the AVS avoidance system in Survey One will engage and she will avoid the guppy, darting to the side or increasing speed, maybe even suddenly dropping a hundred feet."

"Understood, Technical. Guppy One, did you copy?"

"Yes, sir."

"Captain, we need some precision flying here. If you trigger their avoidance system with it damaged, we may never catch them."

"Understood, sir. We'll do our best."

The pilot watched his distance readout. When it indicated 150 feet, he looked at the proximity indicator; it read 12.2 feet-per-second. He backed it down to 12, and then focused on the rear hard point of the Survey Shuttle.

The guppy grew larger and larger. The attention of Survey One's crew was glued to their rear-view monitor. They saw the ramp of the guppy lower, and then the upper door raise to full open. Inside were two suited figures. They hooked tethers to themselves, picked up grappling equipment, stepped to the end of the cargo bay, and then out onto the ramp, and waited. The guppy gradually closed on the speeding shuttle. Soon, the ramp was close enough that one could have stepped across the gap onto the hull of the survey shuttle. The two suited figures, one telling the distance to the pilot of the guppy, the other reaching with a clevis and locking pin to connect the powerful guppy to the runaway ship. Soon, the tremendously strong grappling cable was secured. The two suited figures retreated into the airlock, then into the cabin of the guppy, and processed into the atmosphere of the ship. They strapped themselves into their seats along with the rest of the crew.

"Colonel," the Pilot of the tethered guppy said, "we are connected and ready to pull the Survey Shuttle to a stop, and then to bring it home."

"Roger, Guppy One, nice piece of flying."

"Yes, sir, reversing power."

The guppy pilot gradually began lowering power. The minute he reduced the power below *1 G*, the power setting of Survey One, the situation reversed. The guppy was now being towed into oblivion by the Survey Shuttle. The guppy pilot adjusted his power setting back to **ZERO**, then into reverse. At that point, the velocity of the Survey Shuttle began dropping. The rotor pod of Survey One sensed the decreasing velocity and automatically increased its output to maintain the set velocity of *1G*. The guppy continued to increase reverse power. The tug of war was on. The contest continued until the rotor pod in the Survey

Shuttle reached its maximum power of *10 G's*. The guppy's twin rotor pods were each at 50 percent. The Pilot increased the power to *plus-one G* and the tethered duo of ships were on their way back to the protection of Cosmos.

Guppy One was decelerating toward Zannia at *1G* and accelerating on a perpendicular course at *10 G's*, in a newly learned piloting skill to keep a runaway shuttle stationary just outside the hangar bay of Cosmos. The crew of maintenance people were tethering the suited figure of Juan Valencia to be transferred to the open airlock of the survey shuttle. Juan had the necessary skills to 'hack' the control computer of the runaway vessel and shut it down. The crew of the survey shuttle, suited and ready, payed out a lifeline to the shuttle bay of Cosmos to tow the programmer to the shuttle for the task. When ready, they began the transfer. Juan allowed himself to feel important for just a little while. The battle going on inside him was ferocious.

When he was safely inside the survey shuttle, the outer door was closed and the air lock pressurized. The inner door was opened and Juan took off his helmet, his thick protective gloves, and then sat down at the computer terminal. He opened a storage compartment under the console and retrieved a keyboard, plugged it into the USB input port. He speed-typed on the keyboard for about thirty seconds, a bogus display of addressing the problem. He then typed in a twelve-digit code. The screen changed to

'**Enter Command**'. The crew shouted victory yeas! Juan notified the guppy that he was in control of the survey shuttle's rotor pod and was going to order it to gradually power down over sixty seconds so the guppy could match the power reduction. He did so, and the guppy kept the survey shuttle in place with very little 'see-saw' movement as the rotor pod went to zero thrust. Cecil quickly took the controls and eased the shuttle into the hangar bay. The guppy followed keeping the towing cable slack. The escort guppy followed suit as maintenance closed the hangar doors and pressurized the bay.

The two crews of the guppies, the crew of the survey shuttle, and the maintenance staff in the hangar bay picked up Juan overhead and began carrying him toward the aft lounge, chanting, *"Hail, hail, the man of the hour!"*

Juan Valencia allowed some more feelings to creep in.

Since the party had begun, Colonel Austin ordered the hull inspection be rescheduled for the next day and to be done by Survey Shuttle Two. Included in the order was the requirement for Juan to analyze the systems on it to ensure the same *accident* didn't happen, as did on Survey Shuttle One.

Jimmy then exercised the best judgement of a Commander and joined the party. As he entered the hall, amid the celebration of Juan's *success*, he noticed Mentar off to the side, with Menvaar whispering to him.

No one could hear him saying, "Father, I have been frequenting the Bridge lately. I need to talk to you about Yaccavan."

Jimmy looked for Melvin to congratulate him too; it was his quick work in Telemetry that got the correct rendezvous instructions transmitted to the guppies, enabling them to make it back to Cosmos in the shortest time possible. But, Melvin was not at the party. Jimmy smiled, *"Workaholic...gotta respect a man with dedication."*

Trainee Quarters
Three decks up – Port side

Melvin had his assistant takeover Telemetry, *saying* he wanted to go to the party. But, he was now on the Trainee deck, looking for Space 2107-3, Juan's room. He wasn't really sure why he was there or what he was looking for. But, there was *something* about the young computer expert that had Melvin concerned. He couldn't put his finger on it...but some of Juan's words and actions and his *behind-the-back* resistance to authority had him questioning the young man having so much access to information and systems, critical to the ship's performance.

He was feeling like a thief as his hand reached for the doorknob. He was not going to be guilty of breaking and entering, but he found that the door was already open, about an inch. That sometimes happened when you swung the door closed too hard…it would bounce back a little. Melvin said, "Hello!" and then gently pushed on the knob…the door swung open.

The room was empty, since Juan was at the party, enjoying the praise for fixing the shuttle system. Melvin wasn't so sure he deserved it…*something* wasn't right.

The room was sparse, like most trainee rooms. The girl trainees usually fixed their rooms up nice, since it would be *home* for eight years. But the guys couldn't care less about decorations. On the small table beside the bed, Melvin saw an open scrapbook…an unusual item in a young man's room. He peeked back out in the passageway; no one was around. He opened the front cover and leafed through the first few pages.

The pages were full of old newspaper articles, mostly about the space program. *"Not unusual for a young man,"* he thought, *"Especially one who volunteered for the Colony."* Most of the articles were over 40 years old. He read some of the headlines:

ASTRONAUT ROGER STAHLS FOUND
ALIVE ON THE MOON
NASA Accused of Coverup
Name of decision-maker unknown

ALAN BREWSTER, FBI AGENT
COMMITS SUICIDE
NASA connections under Investigation

MOON SHIP EXPLODES DURING TEST
Sabotage Suspected

MAN ARRESTED IN MOON SHIP SABOTAGE
Name withheld, pending investigation

Melvin saw numerous other articles, mostly about the space program. *"What young guy doesn't like stuff about space?"* he asked himself. There were some unrelated articles about Computer Competitions and even one about Immigration. But, he had to admit, there was nothing here out of the ordinary, for a young man interested in NASA and space travel.

He closed the scrapbook. *"Maybe I was wrong."* He left the door an inch open, the way he had found it, and headed to the party.

Chapter 25

Alpha Centauri

The two starships reached the telemetric journey's end and came to a stop relative to its launch point. They were between the two suns that comprised Alpha Centauri. At this point, Little One was being orbited by its own planet. Zannia was orbiting a point in space that was the center of mass of the two stars—Alpha Centauri A and B.

The telemetry teams of the two ships, after an impromptu conference with the commanders, set a course for an intercept of Zannia to come to rest 140 miles above Kaavar, its capital city.

The Spaceport—Zannia

Little One and Cosmos would arrive in six weeks. Kronos stood on the now-completed addition to Zannia's Spaceport. He thought about taking his first official presidential act; well, *acting* presidential act, and giving the Spaceport an official name. Nothing so bold as Kronos Spaceport, at least not until he had conferred with Mentar and parliament, although he had been running the government for seventeen years.

"So," he mused, "let's just call it *The Spaceport*, for now."

Preparations were being made to welcome the colonists from Earth. They would disembark Cosmos here at The Spaceport, then take a stroll, a two-mile stroll, to Little One Village; a leisurely stroll for a citizen of Zannia. However, it would be a bit of a challenge for a *little one.* Kronos would have rest stations with refreshments set up for them at a couple of locations along the path.

After eight years of confinement on Cosmos, they would certainly be elated with the open blue sky, the trees, the warm sunshine, and fresh air. They would be motivated and jubilant, but their stamina would be down, due to the relative inactivity. Kronos remembered his months of physical therapy to regain his strength following his tenure of service in the light gravity of the moon. Rest stations would be a prudent gesture. However, the colonists would soon snap back and life would begin anew. There would be a brand-new world to come to know.

Six weeks later

Little One and Cosmos appeared above Zannia's recently-enlarged Spaceport and paused at 5000 feet. Cosmos' bridge crew looked downward and scanned the surrounding area in awe. Scattered around within viewing distance were clusters of saucer shaped buildings, city-size in numbers, that seemed to be hovering above the almost total tree-cover of the planet. Closer observation revealed that the cities and towns were supported above the trees by enormous columns, one under each structure. Zannians lived and worked above the trees.

The Spaceport was on the ground, which, considering the concentrated weight of the starships, it would make sense. The spaceport was located in a clearly defined, several miles square, opening in the trees.

Kronos, the members of Parliament, and above a thousand Zannians looked upward when the two starships appeared overhead. They slowly descended and touched down, equalized the pressure, and then opened the two ramps in unison.

Mentar changed his radio frequency for a local call. "Peak Island, this is Mentar, send a message to Earth. Say that Earth Colony – Zannia, has arrived and all is well."

Peak Island replied, "Roger, Mentar, welcome home. Your message will be transmitted immediately."

The two flight commanders of the ships came down the ramps and headed for Kronos' welcoming committee. Momentarily, the people began streaming from the ships. A group of teenagers among the colonists were chattering among themselves as they disembarked, looking up at the sky and around at the huge buildings and enormous trees in the distance.

Suddenly, one of the teens stepped to the side when he was off the ramp, got to his knees, bent over and kissed the ground, then looked up as his colleagues and grinned. He was the rambunctious type. He had boarded Cosmos at age eight. Two years into the journey, he was caught in the engine room hiding among the rotor pods with a fresh tomato in one hand and a salt shaker in the other. Here, six years later, when he raised up from his show of affection to solid ground, scattered laughter rippled through the flow of people.

Kronos, noticing the youngster's gesture, smiled to himself. That had been the way he had felt when that original twenty-two-year journey from Earth aboard Little One was finally over. However, he had resisted the urge for the appearance of dignity. He then stepped onboard Little One and approached Mentar. In a planet-Earth gesture, he extended his hand. "Welcome home, Mentar."

Mentar eyed his hand momentarily, then took it and smiled. "Earth people can get under your skin, can't they. How's everything here on Zannia?"

"Routine. The additional clearing is finished and planted. The population has grown three percent. Things are going well."

"Good." Mentar looked at the disembarking flow of colonists. "Today we start a new era. Some exciting times ahead, Kronos."

Kronos glanced toward the colonists as well. "Several of our manufacturing companies have volunteered to scale down the needed items for Little One Village. It's almost completely stocked and ready for occupation. We've picked a liaison to work with the *little ones*, to determine what the remaining needs are."

Mentar and Kronos were silent for a few minutes as the last of the people exited the starships. Outside, the colonists and scientists had begun to group and examine their surroundings.

As Kavientar was off-loading the *object,* he approached. "Mentar, with your permission, I will store the *object and module* in the Archives Safe Storage Room. The hangar bay workers will show me where it is."

Mentar nodded. "Yes, of course; a good place for it."

After a few steps, Kavientar turned back. "It is interesting that the pulse-frequency of the lights circling the end of the object has been slowly increasing, the last few months. They've increased 10 percent since we recovered it."

Mentar thought for a moment. "I guess that means we are a little closer to whatever star system it came from."

"Yes, perhaps, but I didn't expect such an increase in such a short distance. We'll try to figure it out, once everything settles down." He departed.

Mentar retrieved the Ship's Log from his Bridge Desk, and then walked slowly toward the exit.

"Kronos," Mentar said, "I have a book, a novel, I want you to read. It was given to me by a friend, on Earth."

"A book?"

"Yes. It's called *Gulliver's Travels.*"

"Who's Gulliver?"

"A fictional character somewhere between us and the *little ones*."

Little One Village

The brighter of the two suns would be setting in two hours and the other, a half an hour later. The interim time had become known as *dream time*; conclude your day and plan your evening. When the second sun went down, the cities, due to Solar Mechanical Lighting, would automatically illuminate like floating lily pads on the tree tops. The next morning, as was the case every morning on Zannia, the brighter sun would rise in the northeast, and then, half an hour later, the lessor sun in the southeast and add its lumens to the Zannian day.

Every citizen had two shadows, one pointing southwest, the other northwest. Everyone was a portable sundial that not only told the time, but was also a reference for direction. In between the two shadows, was west, or east.

The giants lined the pathway from The Spaceport to the foundation and the base of the column of Little One Village. The two bridge crews took the lead to begin the two-mile journey to the newly-constructed outpost on Zannia. The 300 colonists, plus the several additions that were born in route from Earth, along with the 96 researchers, began the trek to the permanent home of the colonists and temporary base of the researchers. Many, after almost a mile walk, welcomed the tables and chairs grouped beside the path and the refreshments supplied by their hosts. They soon resumed their march. Upon arriving at the base of the giant column, three hundred feet in diameter, in a cleared area a thousand feet in diameter, they noted the several support structures; utilities, air conditioning, and maintenance for the village at the top of the pedestal.

The giants explained the three elevators, each fifty feet square, located just inside the column, equidistance around it and the in-between access doors to an emergency spiral staircase in the middle of the column. The colonists entered the elevators fifty at a time and went up to their lodgings.

Jimmy stepped off the elevator with the first group to enter the enclosed structure, perched 300 feet into the sky. The main floor had a fifty-foot ceiling. The volume seemed enormous. There were multiple stations where an elevator went upward, presumably to all the floors above; the private apartments. There were also sets of stairs next to each elevator. Scattered across the main floor were sitting areas, lounging type furniture, and tables and chairs. He saw three that were constructed to accommodate giant-*little one* conferences. The colonel and several of his bridge crew went to the nearest elevator, entered and pushed the button for **Floor 2**. The elevator rose smoothly to the second floor. They exited into a lobby area. Six halls led away from it in a wagon wheel-spoke pattern. He stepped down one of the hallways and opened the first door. It was a nicely furnished four-room apartment. Pushing an inner door open and sticking his head in, he saw furniture, complete with bedclothes and all.

"Nice," Colonel Austin said. "We are going to have to take a fresh look at Mentar City to keep up with the Jones, ah, Zannians."

Several of the bridge crew chuckled as they re-entered the elevator.

Standing on the ground at the base of the column, waiting their turn on the elevator, some of the research scientists stepped back to the edge of the clearing and looked upward and examined the *golf-tee* appearing structure. The column went up and just above the tops of the trees and connected to a saucer shaped building a half-mile in diameter. Every fifty feet up the column, there was a platform that circled it. It was fifty feet wide with tables and chairs and some types of structures not identifiable. There was a banister four feet high around its perimeter. Two or three of the onlookers made a guess—places to sit outside; maybe even cook out? Another scientist made an observation. "Using those platforms, the way they are spaced, an agile giant could climb this column."

Settling In

Two of the guppies, laden with the personal belongings of the colonists and researchers, ascended above the trees. They were delivering enough of the needed supplies to accommodate the newcomers for the first night.

When the ships reached five hundred feet above the treetops, Little One Village came into view two miles away. The half-mile diameter saucer-shaped structure had three landing pads jutting out from its perimeter, spaced at equal distances around it. They headed for the nearest one. Some of the people were already standing outside. They landed the guppies and opened the cargo bay doors and the unloading began.

DAN HOLT & MAX HOLT

Chapter 26

The Tour

Jimmy, standing on the landing pad of Little One Village a hundred feet above the treetops, watched a flock of birds circle Cosmos in the distance and land in one of the three-hundred-foot trees, fading the towering sea of green to black. They then rose back into the air as a black cloud and moved on. Their wingspans must have been ten feet or more.

He looked down at the treetops. In fantasy, he imagined dinosaurs roaming through them, consuming the underbrush as they lumbered along. They weren't there of course. The animal kingdom here on Zannia was very similar to that on Earth, except for the size. A curious thing though; there was no rule that said animals had to be the same size on all planets. After all, he knew of one place on Earth that sported animals of smaller general size than the rest of the planet—the fascinating Madagascar. Why? Nature did not always give her reasons—just her tantalizing puzzles.

The ship's crew, the colonists, and the researchers were unloading Cosmos of the belongings and equipment they had brought from Earth. They would be several days getting everything in place. Colonel Austin and crew were being given a preliminary tour of Zannia during the interim. Kronos would be arriving in one of the giants' shuttles momentarily. Mentar was busy giving the Elders a verbal tour and settling them into life as citizens instead of rulers. It made very little difference to them. Things got awkward only during matters political, while adjusting to majority rule. All had a voice by vote. Mentar whispered an Earth axiom. *"Time heals all wounds."*

Kronos' pilot eased the giants' shuttle down on the landing pad and opened the outer doors. Colonel Austin peered into the craft. Two of the giants' seats had been removed and six human-sized seats had been installed. Accenting the change, a set of steps went from the deck up to the raised floor.

Colonel Austin, Bruce Wilson, Timothy Dalton, Kathrine Baylor, Sharon Millar, and Melvin Faulkner filed up the steps and took their seats. Kronos' pilot, Bayan, watched the *little ones* fasten their belts. He then looked up at Kronos and spoke briefly in Moon. Kronos turned to the *little ones*. "You'd better bring a warm coat; some of this tour will be at higher elevations."

The crew released their belts, hurried back into their respective dwellings and returned with jackets in hand.

Kronos smiled and nodded toward Bayan. "Peak Island."

Bayan ascended to 2000 feet and then rotated the shuttle into the lessor sun and began forward flight.

Kronos, sitting to the right of the special seats, leaned forward and eyed the crew from Earth. "Peak

Island is where our interplanetary communications equipment is located. We have three radio telescopes on top of the western peak. One is always aimed at Earth. Also, we have three observatories on the eastern peak. Zannia is now a tropical planet with frequent rains and overcast skies. Mount Peak, actually two peaks about a mile apart, reaches above the clouds for clear *seeing*."

The shuttle passed from the green carpet of trees to the vastness of the ocean. It could well have been the Atlantic or the Pacific on Earth. It looked the same. Barely discernable waves marched in unison toward the East. Several miles rolled by before Bayan began a gradual climb. The twin peaks of Peak Island emerged from the ocean at the horizon. Very quickly, they grew in size until the shuttle was two miles above sea level and beginning to level out. Soon, the crew of Cosmos saw the radio telescopes on the mountain top.

As the shuttle came closer, Jimmy glanced at his crew. "Oh, my God! Those bowls must be a quarter-mile across!"

Bayan circled the three telescopes slowly, then turned toward the twin peak a mile away. The three domes were on a massive scale as well. Katy glanced around at her fellow crewmates. "We are on a planet of giants, you know.'"

Colonel Austin looked up at Kronos. "Can you see Earth with those telescopes?"

"No. However, you can see your sun."

"Can we take a look. It's a chance to see our sun from afar."

Kronos keyed the ship's radio and spoke in Moon. A moment later the nearest observatory began a rotation on its base. Bayan landed the shuttle and opened the doors. The cooler air quickly invaded the ship. The crew from Earth released their belts and donned their jackets.

Colonel Austin climbed up the moveable ladder and peered into the six-inch diameter aperture of the giant's telescope. It was a star field. The one in the center was brighter than the host of stars around it. He returned to the floor and Kronos pointed at a computer monitor. The same spread was displayed there.

"We are not special, are we?" Jimmy said. "It looks like just another star."

"I think that star is special," Kronos responded. "It's supporting life on planet Earth. I have friends there."

Colonel Austin looked up a Kronos. He was smiling.

The remainder of the crew filed up the ladder and gazed at their home across 25 trillion miles of space. It had a quieting effect on them. The distance seemed forever and they were looking toward home from the closest star.

The crew re-boarded the shuttle, removed their jackets, and buckled their seat harnesses. Kronos spoke: "The next thing I want you to see is our space elevator. Bayan, take us there and to the lab."

The shuttle rose from the surface and headed back to the mainland. The colonel and crew saw the shoreline ahead. As with all oceans, the salt water had arranged a sandy beach. At a uniform distance from the water, along the ocean's edge, the tree-line began. It was so prolific that it appeared to have been deliberately planted, cultivated, and tended religiously. The trees were so thick that it would be a magnificent delight for a tree-climbing youth.

Bayan, descending to a thousand feet, turned to the right and followed the shore line for almost an hour. Up ahead, the crew saw a cove jutting up into the forest on the left. Bayan steered the shuttle up into the inlet. It became evident that the cove was a river from inland, flowing into the ocean. Bayan rotated the ship so the windshield was facing the shore where the river met the sea and landed on the sandy river bank.

Kronos pointed at the scene ahead. The crew saw fish jumping out of the water, spreading membrane-type wings and flying twenty to thirty feet and re-entering the water. They flapped their wings like a bat. Sporadically, one would leave the water and fly into the distance until out of sight.

"Apparently, they have longer flight capabilities than their counterparts on Earth," Katy observed. "Our flying fish don't flap their wings; They accelerate out of the water and spread their wings and glide relatively short distances, however, some up to three or four hundred yards."

Outside, there were hundreds of them, flying and then treading water for a couple of minutes while flapping their wings for lift.

"I wanted to show you one of our points-of-interest while we have lunch," Kronos said. He then opened a compartment and retrieved six wafers of oatmeal-looking food and handed one to each crewmember. They each sampled it.

"It's something like an energy bar back home," Katy said, as she began to indulge and watch the one-to-two-foot long flying fish churning the water where the fresh met the salty.

Kronos, watching the phenomenon through the windshield, spoke with adventure in his voice: "We are watching this closely. Someday, they will be leaving the water behind and taking to the skies.

The shuttle rose from the river bank and turned inland and climbed to a mile in altitude. Soon, the crew saw the towering space elevator. At first it looked like a latticework bridge support that got gradually smaller the higher it went. Bayan began a sixty-degree climb. Moments later he reached over and keyed the controls to pressurize the ship. Colonel Austin's ears popped. He swallowed to induce an internal pop to equalize the pressure. He noticed the rest of the crew engaging in the same solution.

Zannia, in its entirety, became visible through the bottom viewport. The first sphere above, with the tower running through it, was still a pin-dot out through the top viewer, as they approached. Kronos was giving a discourse on the tower as the miles rolled by during the climb, citing the records that had been discovered on Earth's moon as well as what was recovered on Zannia shortly after their return to their home planet.

The Lab

The sphere was growing is size. Soon, a second sphere came into view miles farther out in space.

"The counterweight," the crew chimed. Kronos glanced upward. "You better check you belts and harnesses, you will be weightless shortly."

The shuttle gradually slowed its ascent and came to a halt, relative to the thousand-foot-wide orbiting sphere. The weightless crew stared at the scene out the windshield and through the huge window of the lab.

The scientists inside the orbiting lab were all standing on the ceiling. They noticed the shuttle outside the window and several of them waved at Kronos. He waved back. Colonel Austin and crew looked up a Kronos. He smiled, "We use the anti-gravity cubes to cancel the effects of gravity on the lab. It results in the centrifugal force of its circular orbit giving it gravity directed away from the center of Zannia. The scientists have a comfortable environment for their research on space."

"What kind of research," Bruce asked.

"The fabric of space."

"The fabric of space!" Timothy joined in, "I read a book about that a few years ago: it was written by a scientist named…Green, I think. Space is not empty, as one would think."

"Right," Kronos stated. "They are working on improving long range, planet-to-planet, communications. The term most often used is, Quantum Communications. The theory says if we can find out how to connect with the fabric of space, all transmissions would be everywhere in space instantly, just like using your mobile communicator. When you dial a specific number, the signal goes to all other communicators within range. All of them ignore the signal because the number doesn't match, except, of course, the one you are calling. That will be one of the mysteries to solve; how do we isolate the signal we want to hear. The only delay would be for the equipment to glean the signals, in whatever form they are, and put them in understandable code. We have high hopes. Just think, being able to call Earth, like talking to someone across town."

"I hope they find the answer," Colonel Austin said.

"Okay," Kronos said. "Let's return to Little One Village. It will be after the suns have set when we arrive. Tomorrow, I'll show you Zannia's food growing system and her animal kingdom."

Cosmos' bridge crew noted the position of the two suns of Zannia, then watched the planet grow in size rather quickly as Bayan, obviously a skilled and seasoned pilot, accelerated down toward the atmosphere and then on down toward the surface. The ship's velocity reached ten thousand miles per hour in the descent. Bayan masterfully reduced the speed to enter the atmosphere, then set course for Kaavar and Little One Village.   The shuttle passed the two terminators, the first into a two-thirds reduction of light, and then into night.   Ahead was the pedestal city hovering solidly above the treetops, contrasted by a four-square-mile denuded space, abuzz with lights and activity. The shuttle cruised to the personal pedestal of the *little ones* and landed. The crew released their belts and got to their feet.

"Don't forget your jackets," Kronos said.

They all looked up at him, as if they had just finished a ticketed tour.

Kronos smiled. "See you in the morning." His shuttle rose off the landing pad and slowly flew into the darkness.

Colonel Austin looked across the sea of lights, seemingly hovering above the huge plush trees, then up at the stars, winking on and off between the scattered clouds. The night was getting cool. He and his crew made their way inside and to one of the lounges.   The image of the sun and its invisible planetary system, that he had seen through the giants' huge telescope, formed in his mind. "If you didn't know where it was, you could search for a million years without finding it," he mused. "Just another star; but special; it's home."

Colonel Austin and crew were up, dressed, and sitting outside on the landing pad at a table near the

227

building's entrance doors when the first sun peeped above the treetops. They were wearing their jackets during the coolness of the morning, before the sun began its warming of the planet. They'd have to come off soon after the sun cleared the horizon. In half an hour, Kronos and Bayan, in their special shuttle, arrived.

"Good morning," Kronos said, "how did you sleep?"

"Out like a light," Colonel Austin said. "It would be easy to get used to this planet."

They boarded the shuttle and Bayan lifted off and headed toward the opposite point of the compass from the previous day. The panorama across the width of the windshield was an endless jungle of the trees, plush and green. Several miles from the city, Bayan slowed the ship and descended to treetop level and flew slowly along. Here, the trees were spread out from each other. There seemed to be about fifty percent coverage of the land as versus the thickness of the jungle around the city.

"Here," Kronos said, "the jungle is thinner by a half or so for several hundred square miles. The two suns provided almost total coverage of the ground with plant-feeding sunlight because of the different angles of the sun's rays. Animals favor this part of the planet, especially the larger ones. However, they roam almost the whole planet and frequent the rivers and streams. You'll see them shortly."

The crew began searching the trees for a look at extraterrestrial animals, at least from Earth's perspective. Soon, the reward came. On the ground, there were herds of animals closely resembling cattle, horses, and a general variety of goats, sheep, deer, and antelope. Once, Colonel Austin thought he saw a unicorn. "You've got to be kidding me," he said as they all stared. However, closer inspection revealed that it was a light slender version of a rhino with zebra-like markings. It would take a close study to make definite comparisons. Here, an antelope was the size of a moose on Earth. And, likewise with the rest of the animal kingdom.

"Interesting," Sharon remarked.

They also noticed different varieties of fowl, following the animal herds, enjoying the bits of grass, seeds, and plant roots left in their wake.

"This is a general sampling of the animal life on Zannia, along with the fact that there are thousands of species of flying creatures in the trees," Kronos began. "You may have noticed that there are no predatory animals. They were hunted to extinction in a last-ditch effort to get the food supply, principally meat at that time, restored. They were too late."

The shuttle rose from the treetops and headed south. Kronos addressed the crew again. "Now, I want to show you the garden, or perhaps you would call it a farm. It's a ten-square-mile clearing in the trees for growing food and fibrous plants for industrial uses, clothing, etc. We just put in the second one to accommodate our growing population."

The two giants' gardens came into view. There were miles of lush green plants protected under a mesh-type wire wall all around the entire garden. Also, the top was covered by a mesh to keep out the birds and climbing creatures. It was dotted with perfectly-spaced supports over the entire garden. There were several support buildings on each of the sides.

Kronos spoke with conviction: "This time we will be monitoring the balance of life here on Zannia very carefully."

Chapter 27

The New Home

Mentar soon commissioned the Elders to reassemble their cargo ships, now tucked away in Little One's cargo hold, on Zannia's four-square-mile tarmac surrounding the spaceport. He assigned them teams, gleaned from the young on Zannia, both giant and *little ones*, to assist in the task. Menvaar even volunteered…he wanted to be just *one of the kids*. He didn't want the others to see him as, somehow, privileged, being Mentar's son. The youths were delighted. The welcomed him as one of the crowd. They had energy, motivation, and curiosity, sparking a million questions.

The days would roll by. The social life on Zannia would begin developing, and the vehicles of transportation would begin coming together. After a job done, and a brief holiday, the most elderly of the Elders would retire to the university and begin teaching the young. The remaining seasoned scientists would begin the tedious task of finding out how planet Zannia recovered from such abuse, that it was almost lost, becoming a barren desolate wasteland. And, what exactly was the abuse that went undetected until it was too late for the masses of people, forcing them to flee into the cosmos.

Kronos handed the scepter of the government back to Mentar and got involved in helping the scientists get organized to address the planetary issues regarding its environmental health. He also made himself available to the colonists. They would take some time, adjusting to permanent residence on Zannia. They were working on ways to contribute to Zannia, now their home

Mentar spent some time catching up on government matters. There were several issues that Parliament had addressed that were routine. One, was very timely. They had expanded on official references to Zannia's suns, and given them separate designations, pending Mentar's endorsement. They had recommended that, hereafter, the brighter sun be referred to as **Zannia A** and the lessor sun be referred to as **Zannia B**. Mentar signed it and it was included in all records and textbooks, including those the Colony would use to train their young.

Little One City

Jack and Brenda Owenby, the chosen leaders of the Earth Colony, Zannia, were busy setting up all aspects of the colony. The colonists had come to respect them as mature professionals who could be trusted to always do what was right for the majority of the people. It was no surprise when, at the first Colony meeting, the people unanimously voted them in as the Co-Mayors of Little One Village. That status gave them a seat on Mentar's Governing Council. Their first action on the Council was to request Little One Village be granted *city status*, with its name being changed to Little One City. The Council immediately approved the request. The giants would learn quickly why the colonists had such faith in their leaders' wisdom and integrity.

At sixty years old, Jack and Brenda were the eldest of the colonists, and the most qualified to provide the needed leadership. Like most colonists, they had sacrificed a lot to be the *first* to break with the earth and create real *community* on another planet. They had left behind a son and a daughter and three beautiful young grandchildren; that were the hardest part of the decision to go.

But, planning ahead, they had liquidated all of their assets and set up a Family Fund for those they left on Earth. Based on age, marital status and family connections on Earth, the government had paid each colonist an amount of money to clear their financial commitments and provide for those they were leaving behind. Jack and Brenda had been awarded five million dollars, to use as they saw fit, to clear any debts and provide for relatives they would leave behind.

They put that money into their Family Fund. With the combined value, they set up a guaranteed Education and Training Plan that would ensure all current and future grandchildren would have a fully paid education in any field they chose. Their stated *hope* was that some of the kids would grow up and graduate in fields that would be highly valued in the Earth Colony on Zannia, and that they would someday step off of a star ship at Little One City, into the arms of their grandparents. They were encouraged that the President had established a Study Group to determine the feasibility of annual starship departures back and forth between Earth and Zannia. Zannian engineers were still working to improve propulsion and protection systems for star ships, enabling them to reduce even further the transit time between the two worlds.

The international community was invited to participate, including financing for additional star ships. Russia was the first country to make the commitment. Additional ships would increase the possibility of reconnecting with family. Also, Earth entrepreneurs were interested in establishing trade with the giants, especially for the Zolaadine Ore being mined there. As a metal, its strength was far above anything on Earth.

During the eight-year trip to Zannia, Brenda had suggested that she and Jack set a schedule of splitting their sleep time, so that one of them was always awake to handle any issues that may arise. Their schedule was nine months asleep and fifteen months awake. That way, they had months together, where they could work together to resolve issues and conflicts among the colonists. Brenda's counseling skills were invaluable.

In addition to counseling the teenagers who had used the R-bots to race around the rotor pod maintenance corridor, she was able to help two married couples through difficulties that could have led to divorce.

Brenda also did the pre-marriage counseling for a couple who got engaged the last year in route and would be married soon after arriving...having asked Colonel Austin to officiate.

Jack's city planning skills were in immediate need. The giants who built Little One City had not planned ahead for population growth in the colony. Jack's experience told him he would not have long to prepare for the change in population that was sure to happen. At some time in the future, Little One City would also need an organized economy, more sophisticated than just the barter system they would start with.

One evening, Jack and Brenda were spending some time together out on the platform attached to the side of their city. They were discussing the next steps necessary to move the colony forward. As Jack looked over the railing at the lush canopy of trees, he looked at Brenda and smiled. "Well, it looks like I finally got put up on a pedestal."

She smiled back, "Don't let it go to your head. By the way...you forgot to take out the trash."

Three months after their arrival on Zannia, Cosmos' regular compliment began almost daily excursions around the planet to learn all they could about this lush tropical world. They used various shuttles and the guppies as excursion vehicles. The general size of everything was puzzling. There seemed to be no reason why things Zannian were sizable, as were the occupants of this celestial body. Some of the scientists had begun to dig into the reason. One interesting discovery was the presence of an previously-unknown enzyme in Zannian soil, that was also detected in all plants in the garden. Microscopic analysis had shown an accelerated cell-multiplication process. More study would be needed.

Some had done such research on Earth, upon discovering the mysteries of Madagascar. Here, though, the issue was exaggerated. The scientists suggested to Jack and Brenda that, for the next six months, half the colonists would eat only the provisions brought from Earth and the other half would eat Zannian food. The leaders agreed. The colonists then began to measure themselves carefully and accurately, keeping careful records to see if their growth, as well, would be affected by the atmosphere on Zannia.

The first three months on Zannia, the colonists had been working hard to organize and focus on how to establish a routine that would help them adapt to their new life. As often happens in a group of *strangers* thrown together, some misunderstandings arose, tempers flared on occasion and arguments had to be settled.

One day, after *yet another* counseling session to settle a disagreement, Brenda came to Jack with an idea. "Everyone seems on edge from working too hard.

I shouldn't have to be doing this much counseling this early in the game. I think we all need a break."

Jack agreed. He had even had a disagreement or two with the giants who didn't understand why Little One City would need to be expanded at all. He asked her, "What do you have in mind?

"Only the leaders and research scientists have gotten a full look at Zannia. I think the colonists need a full view of this lovely planet, that's going to be our home forever. So, I suggest we commission Colonel Austin to let us all board Cosmos, for about a week's vacation, and take a grand tour of Zannia, from pole to pole. We need to see everything. Maybe we could even stop, get off, and enjoy some of the different terrain on the planet. I wouldn't mind swimming in the ocean at the equator and maybe having a snowball fight at the North Pole…something like that."

Jack smiled, "Great idea. As I recall you are pretty good with a snowball. Remember this?" He raised his hair to show the small scar on his forehead."

Brenda laughed. "Yeah, I remember. As I recall, we made up later."

Colonel Austin and Mentar were approached with the idea and both approved it as a great way for a *time out* for the colonists. Kronos, interested, joined the outing.

With the whole colony back on Cosmos, she set sail for the South Pole. Arriving after both suns had set, the ships windows were lined with *little ones*, getting their first look at Zannia's *Southern Lights*. Earth's Northern Lights were no match for what Zannia's double suns created, as the double light sources bent their rays around the planet. The thick cold atmosphere over the Pole diffused the light into a brilliant *dance*, displaying hundreds of variations of light. The strip in Las Vegas had never displayed anything close to what those looking out the windows saw.

Hovering in the midst of the *greatest show on Zannia*, their first evening meal was a feast, from the onboard Earth stores, complimented by the most delicious fruits Zannia had to offer. The oranges were the size of basketballs, with the insides being sweeter and more filling than Florida's best. Zannia had a type of carrot that was as red as a cherry and large enough to be used as walking stick.

After the meal, Mentar spoke, to once again remind the colonists how important their contribution to Zannia would be. Colonel Austin thanked Jack and Brenda for their leadership and the idea to organize this *get-away*. He encouraged them to just relax and enjoy this week. He said Cosmos would hover during their overnight sleep and would land on the ice in the morning. He said, "You will not believe the size of their **Polidems**, the Zannia-equivalent of Earth penguins."

On the second day, Cosmos headed to the mountains in the southern region. The colonists caught their breaths when the ship exited a cloud, facing a 60,000-foot mountain. As they circumnavigated the base, they saw animals similar to mountain goats, but the size of elephants, bouncing up and down the slopes. The streams flowing out of the mountains were as large as the Amazon river back home.

There were *oohs and ahs* when Cosmos turned up a large valley with grassy slopes on either side. Several said, *"WOW!"* when a turn in the valley brought them to a 10,000-foot-tall waterfall. The spray form the water hitting the rocks below almost filled the entire valley.

The ship's company enjoyed lunch and the view out the windows. Then Cosmos turned downstream and headed for the ocean. As the terrain leveled, just out of the foothills, they flew over a herd of animals that Mentar called **Rotagans**. They were each 20 feet tall and about 35 feet long. They were galloping along together in a herd of what looked like 100,000 strong. The cloud of dust they were making was visible for miles.

Jack and Benda had joined the others at the windows. Jack, originally from the Tennessee countryside, looked at Mentar. "These look a lot like the horses we have in Tennessee, except a lot bigger."

Mentar said, "Actually, this is a herd of what you would call Shetland ponies. The workhorses our culture used eons ago were a lot bigger than these. Our farming is now done with automation, of course."

Arriving at the ocean shore at nightfall, Jimmy directed a landing on the massive ocean beach and joined everyone for a campfire cookout...the first Mentar had ever seen. It was a remnant of Earth that would not soon die away. There were groups gathered around multiple campfires where Earth campfire songs soon broke out. Mentar and the other giants accompanying the colonists observed the ways of these *little ones* with great interest. Kronos looked at Mentar, "So, this is what we started over 50,000 years ago?"

Mentar nodded and smiled. "Looks like we did good."

Looking out over the ocean, Jimmy saw flashes of lightening in the distance, piercing the darkness. He advised all that it was time to move inside Cosmos. The ship stayed on the beach overnight, allowing the colonists to enjoy the sound of baseball-sized raindrops creating a serenade on the hull of the ship, lulling them to sleep.

The next morning, the colonists were awakened to what sounded like explosions off-shore, with volumes of ocean water bursting into the sky and then crashing back to the surface, like hundreds of individual waterfalls. Many rushed to the windows, to see a pod of hundreds of red and blue-colored whales breaching the surface in leaps of over 500 feet and then crashing back into the ocean. Mentar said they were probably following a school of feeder fish and would soon be gone. Many got dressed and ran outside to watch the spectacle. After a few minutes the pod moved on.

After breakfast, Jimmy announced that they would stay two more hours, for those who would like to have their first swim in a Zannian ocean. Pretty much everyone did. The giants watched with curiosity at the *little ones*, in various stages of undress, plunge into the surf and manipulate their arms in a way that propelled them across the water, without sinking. Most giants just shook their heads. Mentar looked at Jimmy. "We still have a lot to learn about each other."

Leaving the ocean, their next stop was the lush deep rain forest that circled the planet at the equator. Bruce slowed Cosmos to allow a close look at the most massive jungle any had ever seen. The trees topped almost a thousand feet is some places. Different types of birds, some as big as Earth-sized shuttle-craft, flocked by the 10,000s, in massive walls of black from tree to tree. There was almost constant cloud cover and rain.

Mentar pointed. "That forest down there was the first element of Zannia's recovery from total ruin. About a hundred thousand years ago our forefathers had harvested the trees for massive building campaigns. Back then, they used the wood as their primary building material. The problem was, they had no program to replant and rebuild this resource. They didn't realize that it was Zannia's primary source of oxygen. Without proper planning, our population overpowered the planet's ability to support it. As you know, our ancestors gave up on fixing it and headed out to find another planet. Had their ship not become disabled in your solar system, we may have never been linked together."

Brenda said, "I don't wish troubles on anyone, but if they had to break down, I'm glad it was in our solar system. I rather enjoy being a Zannian."

After a night of hovering and sleeping over the biggest jungle imaginable, Cosmos headed for the North Pole. The mountains, covered in snow, were pristine. The glistening snow created a million sparkles on the winter-like landscape.

Jimmy looked down, "Looks like Colorado."

"Yeah," said Bruce. "Times 10."

Mentar leaned in, pointing. "Do you see that flat spot at the bottom of that gentle hill?"

Bruce looked. "Yes. Is there something special about it?"

"Yes, I need for you to land there. I have something I want to show all of you."

Bruce reduced power and was soon resting on the landing gear of Cosmos. He selected, **SURFACE,** as his 'flight level,' in case there was a cavern below, that might collapse under the massive weight of the ship. The flight control system would keep the ship in place, since the surface was recognized as the 'set' flight level.

All were looking out the windows at a vast landscape of snow...nothing else. Soon, they turned their attention to Mentar. Jimmy said, "Okay, what should we be looking for?"

Mentar smiled. He keyed the console microphone. "Guppy One, this is Mentar. Captain, are you ready to launch?"

"Roger, sir, ready to launch for the demonstration."

Jimmy was as confused as the passengers. "Where's the guppy going? What demonstration?"

Mentar was still smiling. "Kronos, bring the gift forward."

Everyone turned to see Kronos approaching the Bridge, with a package, about a foot in diameter and six feet long. He walked up to Jimmy and held the package out for him to take it.

Jimmy stared and then turned to Mentar. "For me? What is this?"

Kronos said, "Gift-giving is not part of our culture but we learned through your television programming that gifts are important in yours. After watching some of your competitions being transmitted visually; WINTER OLYMPICS, I believe they were called, Mentar had me commission our engineers to create these for you."

Mentar added, "Based on our conversations in route to Zannia, these will be important to you."

Jimmy took the package, laid it on the conference table and opened it. "SKIS?! And poles and boots?!"

The colonists all applauded.

Before Jimmy could say anything else, Mentar keyed the mic. "Captain, your passenger will be there in a moment, prepare for departure." He then turned to Jimmy. "I asked your guppy pilot if he could devise a way to tow you up that small hill so you could demonstrate to all of us—snow skiing."

Jimmy's broad grin said it all. "Just watch...I won a Silver Medal in college." He then disappeared through the door.

In about five minutes, Guppy One hovered out of the hangar bay and landed near the small hill. The pilot lowered the ramp of his ship. Jimmy appeared at the end of it, wearing the boots. He dropped the skis onto the snow and stepped into the bindings. The guppy Crew Chief unrolled a long rope with a wooden handle affixed to the end, and then came to a hover.

As the rope tightened, Jimmy bent his knees and was towed about 300 yards, up to the top of the hill. He let go of the rope, looked toward Cosmos, raised both ski poles in the air and then pointed his skis downhill. He was soon doing thirty miles an hour, turning back and forth across the hill, headed right for Cosmos. He slid to within thirty feet of the outer hull, turned sideways and skidded to a stop, covering the first landing pad with a shower of snow.

Jack Owenby, when Jimmy was being towed by the guppy, found some sheets of paper on the Bridge desk and quickly wrote something on two of them. When Jimmy stopped his slide, he looked up at those waving through the windows. He laughed at Jack and Brenda...they were holding two signs that each read...'**10.**'

After one more trip down the hill, Colonel Andrews came back aboard. It was the most fun he had had in years. Katy made him promise to plan a future ski trip for the colonists, before the crew and scientists headed back to Earth at the end of the year. Kronos said he might even be willing to give it a try...with larger equipment, of course.

Finally, Cosmos rose from the snow-filled valley to a thousand feet. As the mothership leveled off and began a gentle flight south, Mentar and Kronos were in a quiet discussion. Presently, Mentar made an announcement. "There's something very special about Zannia that we would like you to know. We are now going to fly to our Space Elevator for those of you that have not seen it's elaborate base and structure, then proceed to fly through the Zolaadine Mountain Range. The discovery of Zolaadine is what made it possible to build a stable, safe, space elevator 30,000 miles high, counting the extended height for the counterweight. This was done by our ancestors many eons ago.

"A note; when we fly through the Zolaadine mountains, you will experience an increased measure of gravity. Each of you will weight 14 percent more than you do now. A 140-pound person will weigh 160. It's the concentration of the ore, Zolaadine. You have the same gravity differences on your earth and moon. They are just so minute that they are not noticeable."

Cosmos set the heading and the colonists watched the forest canopy pass under the ship, with an occasional river or stream augmenting the scenery.

Soon the Space Elevator appeared ahead. Cosmos approached to within a quarter-mile, and then set a circular path around it. It looked similar to the base of the Eiffel Tower, except, it had eight legs of latticework spread like a spider and attached to the surface. The onlookers followed it toward the sky through the giant porthole in the top of the ship. It disappeared into the heavens.

"You can't see the lab," Kronos said. "It's at 23,000 miles. You can schedule shuttle excursions to it and actually enter it for a visit. It's a five-hour trip at almost 5000 miles per hour."

Cosmos then set course for the mountain range. Mentar again reminded the colonists of the gravity change as the ship entered a long valley between two strings of mountains. The onlookers noticed the change in their heaviness on their feet; commenting with each other. "This is weight that will be easy to lose."

Mentar cleared his throat. "Ancient records show that our ancestors hollowed out a couple of mountains for the materials to build the space elevator. It's a good thing they did. The space elevator made it possible for the residences of doomed Zannia, at the time, to build a rudimentary starship and actually escape and survive."

After another day of sightseeing and learning, Cosmos settled back on the tarmac near Little One City. The colonists now had a better understanding of the planet they would call *HOME*.

Chapter 28

The Signal

Mentar's Living Quarters

When Mentar awoke, he prepared for another day of government business. He entered the meal room and found Menvaar already having his fruit and vegetables, as he did every morning.

As was the family custom on Zannia, Menvaar stood and greeted Mentar, but in English. "Good morning, Father."

They both sat. "The sleep was pleasant last night?"

Mentar looked at his son; he usually didn't offer such pleasantries first thing in the morning, especially not in English. "Yes, I slept very well, thank you. And I am glad that your mastery of English is progressing so well." After a couple of awkward glances from his son, Mentar asked, "Son, is there something on your mind?"

Menvaar put down his utensils. "Uh...Father, I know it is not our custom to talk of those no longer alive, but I...uh...have been wondering about my mother. Two nights ago I had a...uh, vision; a dream, I believe the *little ones* call it. I've never had one before...it was quite unsettling."

247

Mentar stopped eating. "Others have had such visions. Tell me about it."

Menvaar began, "In the vision, I was very young. Mother was walking away from our home on Solaris 4, carrying her belongings. My sense was that she wasn't coming back. I ran to the door and called to her. She turned and smiled. She put her things down and waved to me, and said, '*goodbye.*' Then she said I should always remember to do two things…to always love and always forgive."

Mentar could see the stress the vision had caused Menvaar. "Son, you're right about our customs, but let me explain, so your mind will be at ease. Your mother's brother was in the group of spiritualists that split from our society and relocated to Solaris 1, what the *little ones* call Venus. On the occasion in your vision, she was going for a visit to see her brother. She was there when Solaris 4 exploded. All life on Solaris 1 perished during that disaster. Your mother was planning to return and then bring you with her to join me on the moon. I regret that she had not made that clear to you.

"As it turned out, your unplanned decision to secure a ride to the moon for a surprise visit, was the thing that eventually saved your life. I will always be grateful for that happenstance. I will always be grateful for the ingenuity of the *little ones*, that saved us all. I miss your mother. I don't speak of it because that is not part of our culture."

Menvaar looked up. "Maybe that is something we need to learn from the *little ones*."

Mentar nodded, "Maybe you're right."

Menvaar smiled. "What Mother said, about always forgive; I have been thinking…I may have been unfair in my assessment of Yaccavan's actions. In route from Earth, I saw some attitudes and actions of his that made me mistrust his motives and his commitment to our society. I didn't like the way he preferred the company of the *little one*, Juan, instead of interacting with others of us in the school on board Little One. Based on my vision, I may have been too hasty in my conclusions."

Mentar was impressed with the noticeable maturity he saw developing in his son. "So, what are you going to do about it?"

Menvaar thought for a moment. "Since today is Rest-Day, there are no classes. I think I will visit Yaccavan, and apologize for my attitude toward him. I will commit myself to be his friend."

Mentar touched his son's arm. "I am proud of you. That is the mark of a youth approaching adulthood. If your mother were here, this would also make her proud." He stood, "Now, there are decisions awaiting at the office; no rest for the leadership. I will see you at the end of today."

Menvaar finished his meal and headed to the Youth Dormitory where all youth without parents lived. He knocked on Yaccavan's door, but he was not in his room. A neighboring youth told Menvaar that he heard Yaccavan say he was going to Little One City for a visit.

Menvaar took the short walk to the city, knowing Yaccavan was going to visit Juan. But the *little ones* said that they had not seen Yaccavan that day and that Juan had left earlier.

After what Menvaar had said to his father, he resisted the urge to assume the two were up to no good. "Maybe they just took a walk," he muttered to himself. He decided to head up to the most popular place for relaxing hikes; Zolaadine Ridge. The southern end of the Zolaadine Mountain Range ended just north of the city complex. Most of the youth, and even some families, enjoyed climbing up the steep trail that circled the sharp ridge and then stopping at the outcropping overlooking both cities and the valley below. The hundreds of pedestal buildings looked like a forest of mushrooms, sprinkled down the valley.

Beginning the climb, before the road tapered into just one lane, he saw the road branch off toward the Zolaadine Mine entrance. The mine was always closed on Rest-Day. As he passed that fork in the road, something white caught his eye, lying on the dark surface of the road, about 20 yards in the direction of the mine. He was alone, so he turned down that lane to investigate. To him, the paper was small. When he turned it over, it was several shades of brown and had the word, **MARS** written across the middle. Underneath were the words, **Milk Chocolate Bar**. "Earth candy!" he said out loud. "It must have been dropped by Juan." He placed it in his pocket to show his father later. "I wonder what he and Yaccavan are doing at the mine…it's closed."

He continued walking the additional mile, around the other side of the ridge, to the mine entrance. He expected to find the two looking around in the equipment area near the entrance. He thought this would be a good time to apologize to both of them for the way he had been feeling.

When he arrived at the mine entrance, no one was there. Menvaar thought he had been wrong…that they must have continued to the overlook. He decided to check the doors anyway. The two 50-foot-high, 30-foot-wide metal doors appeared to be closed, but upon closer inspection, they were about an inch open, just enough room for him to get a fingernail in the crack. With a little effort, the doors slide apart.

The hundred-foot-high tunnel was dark, with sparse overhead lighting. On days off, the miners only kept 20 percent of the lights on, for safety purposes. The strong distinctive odor of Zolaadine filled his nostrils. He heard nothing. He knew that even though the doors were unlocked, he was breaking the rules…only miners were allowed inside the tunnels. After walking 50 yards, he turned back toward the door. It was then that he heard the noise; something metal, sounded like it had been dropped from a height and had bounced on the tunnel floor.

Menvaar hurried toward the sound; it was coming from a side tunnel. He heard a voice that he was sure was Yaccavan's. As the metal object bounced again, the voice yelled, "RUN…RUN!"

The next few moments seemed like slow motion. The explosion was so sudden the Menvaar was knocked on his back. The impact of the pressure wave made him temporarily deaf and he was being covered in a layer of tunnel dust. Momentarily, his ears began hearing the aftermath of something being blown apart and the shower of rocks resulting from the explosion.

He rolled over on his hands and knees and began crawling toward the site of the explosion. He stayed low to keep out of the thickest part of the debris-cloud and still be able to breathe. The overhead lights had been destroyed so he had to enter almost total darkness.

He called out, "YACCAVAN! JUAN! WHERE ARE YOU?!

At first; nothing. Then, a weak giant's voice said, "Menvaar..we are here. We need help, Juan is hurt badly."

Menvaar crawled toward the voice and found Yaccavan, with a large wooden support beam, laying across his back. He was hovering over Juan, as if to protect him. The young giant was bleeding from his forehead and his shoulder appeared to be broken. Juan was laying on his back, covered in dirt and dust. Blood was flowing from his left side, puddling underneath him.

He lifted the beam off Yaccavan and threw it aside. "Yaccavan, what happened?"

"We...uh...we caused the explosion."

"WHAT?! WHY?!"

"Menvaar, we need help right now! Please, go to the Emergency Communicator in the next tunnel and alert the Mining Office." He looked down at Juan. "I'm…I'm afraid Juan might die. Hurry!"

Menvaar got to his feet and ran through the cloud of dust to the adjacent tunnel. He alerted the Mining Office and asked them to dispatch an emergency medical unit to the mine. He then ran back to see what he could do to help. Yaccavan was just exiting the side tunnel with Juan in his arms. His tunic was already soaked with Juan's blood. He looked down at Juan. "It will help to meet them at the door. Juan can't make it much longer."

Mentar and Jimmy were both alerted, along with Jack and Brenda and the Colony Doctor. They all met at the giants' medical clinic, at the bottom of the ridge, where it met the edge of the city. When they rushed in, Brenda and the doctor ran to the giants attending Juan. Mentar saw Yaccavan, lying on a table, being attended to. Menvaar was standing nearby, covered in dirt. Mentar looked him over. "Are you alright, son? What were you doing in the mine? Did you cause the explosion?"

"Father…I…"

Yaccavan interrupted. "Mentar…sir, Menvaar had nothing to do with the explosion. Juan and I were at fault. Menvaar was looking for us when the explosion happened. He is the one who found us and helped save us." He looked over at the table where they were trying to save Juan's life. "Juan is injured very badly. I fear he may not live."

Juan was unconscious. The Colony Doctor was working with the clinic doctors, trying to stop the bleeding from Juan's side. The explosion had broken his left leg and several ribs. One of them had severed an artery, causing the internal bleeding. He needed a transfusion if he was going to survive. Juan's blood-type was **B+**. The Doctor knew the blood-types of the colony leaders; none had **B+**.

Jack had an idea. He asked the Head of the Clinic; "Back when you were tinkering with *US*, well over 50,000 years ago, did you happen to do any cross-matching of blood-types, to determine compatibility?"

The Head Doctor said, "Why, yes. Actually, your blood-types are derivatives of ours." He turned to his nurse. "Our **CY+** type is compatible. Pull up the records of everyone here in the clinic and see if we have a blood-type match."

Yaccavan rolled over and stood up from his bed. "No need to check, doctor, I have **CY+**. With Menvaar's help, he walked haltingly to Juan's bed. "Just tell me what to do."

The nurse looked at the doctor; he nodded. She said, "Sit in this chair by Juan. Only a small amount from you will meet his requirements."

Soon the transfusion was in process. When Juan's blood pressure recovered to a safe level, they began the operation to repair the broken bones.

As everyone waited, both Jimmy's and Mentar's communicators rang simultaneously. Kavientar had linked both of them together. He sounded almost out of breath as he spoke. "Gentlemen, another Module has been found!"

"What?!" Mentar was staring at Jimmy.

Jimmy responded. "Where?"

Kavientar almost shouted, "In the mine! The explosion blew a hole in the wall, exposing an unknown cavern under the mountain. Inside was another metal box. When they opened it, there was another module, glowing! They left it there and evacuated the mine. At the same time, the Archives Curator called me. The lights on the Object are flashing so quickly that it is producing solid bright light."

Jimmy leaned over, "We need that module. This could be incredible."

Mentar nodded. "Kavientar, take a team and retrieve the module. Take it to the Archives and keep it separate. Do not insert it into the Object until we get there. The colonel and I will meet you there in an hour."

Mentar and Jimmy turned their attention back to the medical emergency. Juan was reviving but still groggy, with his vital signs stabilized. The clinic giants had set the broken leg while the Colony Doctor had repaired the severed artery in his side. The broken ribs would have to heal with just a body wrap and some serious rest.

Mentar took Yaccavan to an adjacent room to have a talk with him.

Jimmy asked for some alone time with Juan.

Juan looked up at Jimmy with obvious tears in his eyes. His voice was labored. "Colonel...I...I'm sorry...uh..."

Jimmy put up a hand. "Juan...just rest for a minute; let me talk. Back on Earth, when Katy told me you had been assigned as a trainee on the Bridge, to learn communications and computers, I resisted. I felt you would just get in the way. And, I saw and heard some things from you and about you that did have me a little concerned along the way. But, I must admit that you are one of the smartest computer guys I have seen and you are a quick learner. When you fixed the damaged navigation codes on the Scanner Shuttle, I was really..."

Juan interrupted, "No, no..."

Jimmy leaned closer, "What do you mean, No? I saw you fix it."

Juan was slowly shaking his head. "I...I didn't fix it...I broke it." He looked into Jimmy's eyes.

"Juan, what do you mean?"

The tears were flowing now. "Sir, my name is not Juan Valencia. As a child I went by Trey." Jimmy started to speak. Juan shook his head. "Please let me get this out." He swallowed and wiped his eyes. "My grandfather was Alan Brewster."

Jimmy's eyes widened. "The one who left Roger Stahls behind on the moon?!"

"Yes, sir. He became an CIA Agent and worked with that secret facility in Nevada to cover up what he and they had done. When those guys that invented that first saucer found the giants and brought Stahls back to Earth, Grandpa knew they would connect him to it. He couldn't take the shame, so he...uh...he..."

"Yes, I know, he committed suicide. I'm sorry you had to learn that about him."

"Sir, there's more. My dad was Alan Brewster Junior. When Grandpa died, Dad swore to get even with the government, so he messed with the rotor pod on one of the new moon-ships they were testing and it blew up on a test run at the Bonneville Salt Flats. Nobody was killed but they accused him of sabotage and sent him to prison for 20 years."

Jimmy could see Juan struggling with his story. He stepped over and got some water for him.

Juan drank and then continued. "After he got out of prison, he met my mother, Juanita Valencia. A couple of years after they had me, she was caught and deported back to Mexico. I can't even remember her. After that, Dad just went downhill, mentally and physically. He had no friends and I was his only family. As early as I can remember, he taught me to hate the government and anyone else who didn't feel the same way. When I was nine, he convinced me to change my name to Juan Valencia, after my mother's name, and to promise to find a way to get back at the government for what they did to him and Grandpa."

"Is that why you applied for a place in the Colony?"

"Yes...it was the best way to get close to something important and to try to mess it up. When I met Yaccavan in Colony School, he seemed to feel the same way because of what their government did to his father. So, we kinda started working together to resist the leadership; to show them…uh…you, that we could do what we wanted. I…uh…sneaked into the hangar and put a virus into the navigation program of the Scanner Shuttle. It was just supposed to jerk the crew around and cause them to cancel the mission. It was just another way to cause a little trouble. But when it almost killed the crew and put the guppies in danger, I got scared that I had gone too far." He looked up sheepishly. "I already had the fix programmed in, so I could just type in a code and be the hero."

Jimmy stared for a long moment. The pause was torture for Juan. Then Jimmy asked. "Okay, if you were feeling bad for the chaos you caused, what was the mine explosion all about?"

"Well, sir, that was actually Yaccavan's idea. After we finally landed, I told Yaccavan that I thought it was wrong to keep causing trouble. He said he wanted to do one last thing to *show* the leaders, and he needed my help. I should have said *NO* then but he is my friend, so I agreed. I still don't like what happened to my grandpa and my dad, but all the hating and getting-even has been getting to me. You and Mentar and the giants and all of the colonists seem to be just normal…everybody doing their jobs, regardless of what the government says or does. I know now, what happened is not anybody's fault here. I just want to be part of everything. I don't want to be Juan Valencia anymore."

Jimmy smiled. "Listen, Juan…uh, Trey…what you just said took a lot of courage. I feel sorry that your family background took away the childhood you could have had. But, you can always start over. Jack and Brenda still have a need for computer experts like you, as long as you have the colony's best interest in mind."

Trey's eyes lit up and he allowed a little smile. "You mean…I can stay…you're not gonna send me back to Earth?"

Another voice came from over Trey's shoulder. "As far as we're concerned, you are welcome to stay."

Trey grimaced a little as he turned to see Jack and Brenda coming from around the curtain. They had been on the other side, listening.

Brenda gently touched his hand. "Jua…uh, Trey, many people go through losses and trauma in their lives. Fortunately, some, like you, realize they are in charge of their own attitudes and living their own lives, regardless of what they've been through. Today is a good start for you. Give yourself some time to heal and you and I will spend some time together."

Jack weighed in. "And, there are some steps to setting up the Colony Admin System that require computer skills way beyond mine. I could use your help."

"Thanks, all of you," Trey said.

He had not been this happy since he was nine.

Across the Clinic, Mentar was looking Yaccavan in the eyes, waiting for an explanation for his actions. He finally raised his head.

"When The *little ones* rescued us from the ocean on Earth, and I was told that my father perished with our civilization, I was very angry. He was a good father and a scientist who should have been selected as an Elder in the government, instead of Jaatine's father. If he had been an Elder, he would have been on the fleet's mission to the moon and would have survived.

"I felt betrayed by my own race and I decided to punish the authorities any way I could, to avenge my father's death. I felt that I could show all of you that there are consequences for disrespecting my father. I thought that damaging the machine that was mining the Zolaadine would do that. I broke the lock on the explosive storage unit and took enough to do some damage. But, I set the timer incorrectly and it exploded as soon as we walked away. It was a stupid thing to do."

He made eye contact with Mentar. "I guess the only good thing I've done in all these years, is to save Juan's life with my blood." He paused and looked toward the door, and then back to Mentar.

Mentar sat back in his chair, preparing his thoughts. He leaned closer. "Yaccavan, your father and Jaatine's father were good friends, isn't that so?"

"Yes, sir."

"Well, who do you think recommended that his father be selected as an Elder?"

Yaccavan stared. "Who...my father?! You must be mistaken!"

"No, I'm not. I spoke to your father myself, after he had written the recommendation. I knew he was next in line, and was the most qualified for the open position. As you know, he was a very private individual, especially since your mother had died years earlier. He was reluctant, but finally shared that he had contracted a fatal disease, from which he would not survive. He wanted his best friend to have the position.

Yaccavan's eyes widened. "Disease? He never shared that with me. Why would he hold that back?"

"I'm not sure, except that he thought he had plenty of time to find the right moment to tell you. Solaris 4 changed all that. I feel he would have told you after the mission to the moon had returned home. He never got that chance. He gave up his rightful place in the government for the greater good of our society. The few of us who knew, considered your father to be a hero. I honored him by choosing you to be the Communications Trainee on my Bridge. It was a way I could respect your father."

Yaccavan was silent. In a moment, there was a knock on the door. Brenda opened it and looked at Yaccavan.

"Trey, would like to see you."

"Trey? Who's Trey?"

DAN HOLT & MAX HOLT

Chapter 29

The Formula

Storage Area – The Archives

Mentar and Jimmy entered the storage area and joined the group that Kavientar had assembled. The object, with the one Module attached, had been lifted onto a large table. The lights circling the blunt end were pulsing so rapidly that it was almost a steady bright glow. A door was open to an adjacent room, where the new Module had been placed, at the most distant end away from the Object. The Module was glowing so brightly, it was almost blinding.

Mentar looked around at everyone there, and then nodded. Kavientar went to the blunt end and lowered his hand to the circular outline, barely visible. As before, the circle of metal dropped inside the Object and then swiveled to the side. The end surface immediately dropped down into the end, creating another cone shape, the size of the end of the Module.

"Bring the Module." At Kavientar's voice, two giants carried the Module into the room. When they got within 20 feet of the Object, the Module was pulled from their grasp and lodged itself into the cone recess.

Everyone jumped back, expecting…*something*. At first, a high-pitched sound could be heard, which grew louder by the moment. Everyone started moving back and covering their ears. Suddenly the piercing sound changed to a low-pitched metallic sound, like lugs being withdrawn from recesses when a metal door is about to open.

Suddenly the noise stopped. In a moment, one entire side of the Object went dark. All were looking at each other. Then, new lights, covering the entire surface of the Object began to flash. It became a bright blinding glow. A sound, like a kettle just beginning to steam, started coming from it. Everyone started moving farther back.

Again, the noise stopped. In a moment, one entire side of the Object folded down, revealing a giant-sized keyboard, with two large buttons, one white and one green, side-by-side, in the center. The remaining keys were representations of some unknown language.

As Mentar approached it, the white button began to flash. He looked around at Jimmy; he nodded. Mentar placed his hand over it and pushed it.

Instantly, the room was filled with a hologram being projected from the button, engulfing everyone. They were all standing in the middle of a star-field; in a spiral arm of the Milky Way Galaxy.

Kavientar pointed to a bright star off to one side. "Bernard's Star."

Jimmy nodded and walked closer to it, squinting at... *something* he couldn't identify. It looked like a tiny part of open space was... warped, leading farther into the galaxy, to another large star that was flashing.

Mentar joined him, "An anomaly," he said.

"A worm hole?"

Mentar hesitated, "Maybe; not sure."

As suddenly as it had appeared, the hologram was gone, instantly replaced by a mathematical formula, hovering in the air. Jimmy moved closer, head back, reading the formula from top to bottom. "I'm a Math major, but this makes no sense."

Kavientar stepped closer. "Read it from right to left!" he said excitedly, then hastily recorded the formula.

Jimmy did…and then his eyes widened. "That's it!"

"That's what?" Mentar asked.

"It's what your scientists and mathematicians, living up in the Space Elevator Lab, are searching for. It's the secret of Quantum Communications!"

The formula disappeared. Mentar turned to the Object. The green button was flashing. He looked around at the others, and then back at the button. He extended his hand and pushed it.

The Journey Continues!

ABOUT THE AUTHORS

Dan Holt is a U.S. Army veteran, having served three years as a Communications Specialist in Germany. He spent the remainder of his civilian career as a self-taught engineer, designing and testing large-scale production equipment for the file folder industry. The efficiency and durability of his designs even garnered interest from some foreign manufacturers.

In retirement, Dan has used his writing skills to express his continuing fascination with science fiction. His variety in sci-fi thought is evident in his other novels, SLEEP MODE and KEEPSAKE. The Underneath the Moon series, Sleep Mode and Keepsake are all now available on audio through www.audible.com. See all of Dan's books at the publisher's website, www.maxholtmedia.com.

Contact Dan through his Amazon Author's Page. https://www.amazon.com/Dan-Holt/e/B012LRN65K/ref=sr_ntt_srch_lnk_1?qid=1491001715&sr=8-1

DAN HOLT

Max Holt is a retired U.S. Army pilot, having served 22 years on active duty, including two combat tours in Vietnam. He is an avid Science Fiction reader and writer. Max started his publishing company, Max Holt Media, in 2015. This book begins Max's partnership with his brother, Dan Holt, to continue writing the UNDERNEATH THE MOON saga, expected to continue for several more volumes. They will also partner in a new series, under development, entitled...AI RISING. The working title for Book One is...THE DOME.

Max and his wife Sandy have two sons and six grandchildren. They enjoy traveling and have collected flags from 37 countries. Other than the USA, their favorites have been Switzerland, Austria, Italy and the UK, where they have established a life-long friendship with a family in Darlington, England. They now live in Mount Juliet, near Nashville, Tennessee.

Contact Max: www.maxholtmedia.com
                    max@maxholtmedia.com
On Twitter - @maxholtmedia

Other Sci-Fi books by Max Holt:
        Alien Planet
Series under development, with Dan Holt
        AI Rising

MAX HOLT

www.ingramcontent.com/pod-product-compliance
Lightning Source LLC
Chambersburg PA
CBHW061602170626
46811CB00001B/288